'Even if I ask you to?'

'Are you asking?'

'Yes, *belezza*  ap-praisal with r____ ____ing my baby. It's th____

'But people don____ ____ just because—'

'In my family they do,' Sergio cut in.

Kathy tried not to grimace as the sensation in her abdomen became definite enough to warn her that she was going into labour. It was a very vulnerable moment, and she fully recognised the fact. He didn't love her, but he was willing to be there for her as the father of her child. Just then that mattered to her as much as the knowledge that if she said yes, he would stay with her.

'Okay…I'll marry you,' she muttered jerkily.

'I'll organise it.' His lean, dark features serious, Sergio's smooth response bore the infuriating hallmarks of a male who had not expected any other reply. 'We'll organise the ceremony before the baby's born—'

'I don't th-think so,' Kathy gasped as another pain rippled in a wave across her lower body, returning stronger and faster than she had expected. 'My contractions have started again. Our baby's going to get here first.'

THE RICH, THE RUTHLESS AND THE REALLY HANDSOME

How far will they go to win their wives?

A trilogy by Lynne Graham

THE DESERT SHEIKH'S CAPTIVE WIFE
THE GREEK TYCOON'S DEFIANT BRIDE
THE ITALIAN BILLIONAIRE'S PREGNANT BRIDE

Three men blessed with power, wealth and looks—
what more can they need? Wives, that's what…
and they'll use whatever means to take them!

Prince Rashad of Bakhar, heir to a desert kingdom,
Leonidas Pallis, scion of one of Greece's leading
dynasties, and Sergio Torrente, an impossibly
charismatic, self-made Italian billionaire. They were
best friends when they studied at Oxford and learnt that
it was better *never* to fall in love. Now, led by passion,
Rashad, Leonidas and Sergio have finally found the
women they want to marry and will use their influence,
pay their money, but keep their emotions firmly under
wraps, to get what they want. Only none has bargained
on being brought to his knees by his chosen wife…
Or having his cold heart melted!

THE ITALIAN BILLIONAIRE'S PREGNANT BRIDE

BY
LYNNE GRAHAM

MILLS & BOON®
Pure reading pleasure

All the characters in this book have no existence outside the imagination
of the author, and have no relation whatsoever to anyone bearing the
same name or names. They are not even distantly inspired by any
individual known or unknown to the author, and all the incidents are
pure invention.

First published in Great Britain 2008
Harlequin Mills & Boon Limited,
Eton House, 18-24 Paradise Road, Richmond, Surrey TW9 1SR

ISBN: 978 0 263 86416 8

Set in Times Roman 10½ on 12¾ pt
01-0408-53033

Printed and bound in Spain
by Litografia Rosés, S.A., Barcelona

THE ITALIAN
BILLIONAIRE'S
PREGNANT BRIDE

CHAPTER ONE

SERGIO TORRENTE walked into the Palazzo Azzarini for the first time in ten years.

A magnificent mansion in the Tuscan hills, the palazzo was as famous for its grand Palladian architecture as for its legendary Azzarini wine label, which had spawned a massive empire with vineyards all over the world. Sadly, recent financial reverses had taken their toll: the breathtaking collection of treasures that had once filled the house was gone and the grandeur had become shabby. But it belonged to Sergio now. All of it. Every stone, every inch of rich productive earth, and he was rich enough to turn the clock back and remedy the neglect.

He had regained his birthright; it should have been a moment of supreme triumph. Yet Sergio felt nothing. He had stopped feeling a long time ago. At first it had been a defence mechanism but it had soon become an engrained habit he nourished. He liked the clean, efficient structure of his existence. He did not suffer from emotional highs and lows. When he wanted something more, when he felt the need for a certain buzz to bring him alive, he got it out of sex or physical challenge. He had climbed sheer rock faces in blizzards, trekked through jungles in appalling conditions and engaged in extreme sports. He had not found fear. But he had not found anything he really cared about, either, he acknowledged grimly.

Sergio strolled through the echoing empty entrance hall at an unhurried pace. Once the palazzo had been a happy place and he had been a loving son, who took family affection, wealth and security for granted. But the fond memories had long since been wiped out by the nightmare that had followed. He now knew more than he had ever wanted to know about the depths of human greed. His strong, handsome features set in forbidding lines, he strolled out onto the rear terrace, which overlooked the gardens. The sound of footsteps turned his head. A woman was walking towards him.

Platinum-blonde hair rippled back from Grazia's perfect face. The white slip dress clinging to her pouting nipples and outlining the mound at the junction of her thighs left little to the imagination: she was naked beneath the silk. Grazia had always known what appealed most to a man and it wasn't conversation. He got the message: it was basic and it was instant.

'Don't throw me out.' Her languorous turquoise eyes proffered an invitation that both teased and begged. 'There's nothing I won't do for a second chance with you.'

Sergio raised a derisive ebony brow. 'I don't do second chances.'

'Even if this time I offer you a free trial? No strings attached? I can say sorry with style.' With a provocative look, Grazia folded fluidly down on her knees in front of him and reached for the clasp on his belt.

For a split second, Sergio was taut and then he vented an appreciative laugh. A consummate survivor, Grazia had the morals of a whore but at least she was honest about it. To the winner went the spoils. And without a doubt she was a prize many men would kill to possess, for she was beautiful, sexually adventurous and an aristocrat born and bred. He knew exactly what Grazia was, as once she had been his. A heartbeat later, however, when his bright prospects were destroyed, she had been his brother's. Love on a budget had had zero appeal for Grazia; she went where the money was. And time had wrought dramatic changes, since Sergio was now a billionaire and the Azzarini vineyards were just one small part of his enterprises.

'You're my brother's wife,' he reminded her softly, angling his lean hips back to lounge indolently against the wall a tantalising few inches out of her reach, 'and I don't do adultery, *cara mia*.'

His mobile phone rang. 'Excuse me,' he murmured with perfect cool and he walked back indoors, just leaving her kneeling in sensual subservience on the tiles of the terrace.

The call was from his security chief, Renzo Catallone, in London. Sergio suppressed a sigh. Once a senior police officer, the older man took his job very seriously. Sergio had a valuable chess set on display in his London office and, a few weeks ago, he'd been startled to see that someone, in blatant disregard of the 'Do Not Touch' notice, had solved the most recent chess puzzle he had laid out on the board. Since then, every subsequent move Sergio had made had been matched.

'Look, if it's bothering you that much, hide a surveillance camera nearby,' Sergio suggested.

'This nonsense with the chessboard is bugging my whole team,' Renzo confessed. 'We're determined to catch this joker out.'

'What are we going to do with him when we catch

him?' Sergio enquired drily. 'Charge him with challenging me to a game of chess?'

'It's more serious than you think,' the older man countered. 'That vestibule is in a private area right beside your office, yet someone is walking in and out of there whenever they like. It's a dangerous breach of security. I checked the board this afternoon but I couldn't tell if any of the pieces had been moved again.'

'Don't worry about it,' Sergio told him gently. 'I will know immediately.'

Not least because he was playing a highly innovative opponent, ready to use a game to attract his attention. The culprit could only be an ambitious member of his executive staff, keen to impress him with his strategic skills.

The young man was so busy staring at Kathy that he almost tripped over a chair on his way out of the café.

'You're seriously good for business.' Bridget Kirk's round, good-natured face shone with amusement. A bustling brunette of forty-one, she was the manager. 'All the men want you to serve them. When are you going to pick one of them to go out with?'

Her green eyes veiled to conceal her awkwardness at the question, Kathy forced a laugh. 'I haven't got time for a boyfriend.'

Watching the youthful redhead pull on her jacket to go home, Bridget suppressed a sigh. Kathy Galvin was drop-dead gorgeous and only twenty-three years old, but she lived like a hermit. 'You could always squeeze one in somewhere. You're only young once. All you seem to do is work and study. I hope you're not worrying about old history and how to explain it. That's all behind you now.'

Kathy resisted the urge to respond that the past was still with her all the time, physically in the shape of a livid scar on her back, haunting her in nightmares and shadowing and threatening her even during daylight hours with a sense of insecurity. She knew now that if you were unlucky you didn't even need to do anything bad to have everything taken away from you. Her life had gone badly wrong when she was nineteen years old. As far as she knew nothing she had done had contributed to that situation. Indeed, when she had been least expecting it, calamity had come out of nowhere and almost destroyed her. Although she had survived the experience it had changed her. Once she had been confident, outgoing and trusting. She had also had complete faith in the integrity of the justice system and an even deeper belief in the essential kindness of other human beings. Four years on, those convictions had taken a savage beating and now she preferred to keep herself to herself, rather than invite rejection and hurt.

Bridget squeezed the younger woman's slight shoulder. It was a stretch for her because Kathy was a good bit taller than she was. 'It *is* behind you now,' the brunette murmured gently. 'Stop brooding about it.'

Walking home, Kathy reflected how lucky she was to work for someone like Bridget, who accepted her in spite of her past. Unhappily, Kathy had discovered that if she wanted to work that kind of honesty was a rare luxury, and she had learnt to be inventive with her CV to explain the gap in her employment record. To survive she had two jobs: evenings as an office cleaner, day shifts as a waitress. She needed every penny to pay the bills and there was nothing left over at the end. Even so, long, frustrating months of soul-destroying unemployment had taught

Kathy to be grateful for what she had. Few people were as generous and open-minded as Bridget. Although Kathy had qualifications, she'd still had to settle for unskilled and poorly paid work.

As always, it was a relief to get the door of her bedsit safely shut behind her. She loved her privacy and relished the fact that she had no noisy neighbours. She had painted the bedsit's walls pale colours to reflect the light that flooded through the window. Tigger was curled up on the sill outside awaiting her return. She let the elderly tortoiseshell cat in and fed him. He was a stray and half-wild and it had taken months for her to win his trust. Even now he would panic if she closed the window, so no matter how cold it was it stayed open for the duration of his visits. She understood exactly how he felt and his health had improved greatly since she had begun caring for him. His coat had acquired a gloss and his thin lanky frame a decent covering of flesh.

Tigger reminded her of the pet cat that her family had once cherished. An only child, Kathy had had a chequered early history. Abandoned by her birth mother in a park when she was a year old, Kathy had been adopted as a toddler. But by the time she was ten tragedy had struck again when her adoptive mother had died in a train crash, and soon afterwards a debilitating illness had begun to claim her father's health. Kathy had become a carer in her teens, struggling to cope with looking after the older man while at the same time running a home on a tight budget and keeping up with her schoolwork. Her love for her surviving parent had strengthened her and if she had any consolation now it was that her father had died before the bright academic future he had foreseen for his daughter had been destroyed.

A couple of hours later, Kathy entered the office block where she worked five nights a week. She had got to quite like cleaning. It was peaceful. As long as she got through her work on time, nobody bossed her about and there were very few men around to harass her. She had soon discovered that hardly anyone paid much heed to the maintenance staff: it was if their very lowliness made them invisible and unworthy of notice, which suited Kathy right down to the ground. She had never been comfortable with the way her looks tended to attract male attention.

As there were still some employees at work, she dealt with the public areas first. Even the stalwarts were packing up to go home when she began on the offices. She was emptying a bin when an impatient masculine voice hailed her from the far end of the corridor.

'Are you the cleaner? Come into my office—I've had a spillage!'

Kathy spun round. The man in the smart business suit didn't bother to look at her before he swung on his heel. As she hurried in his wake with her trolley he vanished through the doorway that led into the swanky private office suite where the pretentious chess set was on display. The 'Do Not Touch' notice was still in a prominent position. Her mouth quirked and her gaze skimmed the board as she moved past. Another move had been made by her unknown opponent. She would make hers during her break when she was the only person left on the floor.

The big office was huge and imposing and it had a fabulous view of the London City skyline. The man had his back turned to her while he talked on the phone in a foreign language. He was very tall with broad shoulders and black hair. Those observations concluded her interest, for she finally spotted the spillage he had mentioned: a porcelain coffee jug with a broken handle that had spread its contents over a wide area. She soaked up the dark liquid as best she could and then went to fill her bucket with fresh water.

Sergio ended his phone call and sat down at his glass desk. Only then did he notice the cleaner, who was down on her knees busily scrubbing the carpet on the other side of the office. The long hair clasped at her nape was an eye-catching metallic mix of copper, amber and auburn shades.

'Thank you. I'm sure that'll do,' he told her dismissively.

Kathy glanced up. 'It'll stain if I leave it,' she warned.

She settled huge green eyes on him. They were fringed with lashes like a cartoon fawn's, Sergio found himself thinking abstractedly. Her face was heart-shaped and unusual and so spectacular in its beauty that he who never stared at a woman stared. Even a shapeless overall could not conceal the grace of her slender long-legged figure. Just as quickly he was convinced that she could not possibly be an authentic cleaner. She had to be an out-of-work actress or a model. Women that beautiful didn't scrub floors for a living. How had she got past Security?

Had one of his friends set him up for a joke? Neither of his best friends was a likely candidate, Sergio acknowledged wryly. It would be too juvenile a trick for Leonidas, and Rashad had become alarmingly unadventurous since he had acquired a wife and children. Of course he had other friends. But it was equally likely that the lady was trying to set him up for her own reasons.

For a split second when she focused on the male behind the desk, Kathy had gawped like a startled schoolgirl because he was a dazzlingly handsome guy. He had gleaming cropped black hair, brilliant eyes like polished jet set below level brows, high sculpted cheekbones and a strong patrician nose. The whole was connected by smooth planes of olive skin that roughened and darkened around his hard jaw line. Her heart slowed to a dulled heavy thud that seemed to get in the way of her breathing normally.

'The carpet?' she framed unevenly, the effort of even remembering the task she had been doing a challenge as she scrambled to her feet, ready to leave.

Sergio was committing her flawless features to memory. Stunning women were not a novelty to him. So, he was still trying to work out what it was about her face that gave it such amazingly powerful appeal that it was a challenge to look away from her. He lounged back in his seat with deceptive indolence. 'Go ahead and clean it,' he urged huskily. 'But before you do, answer one question. Which one of my friends sent you here?'

Her delicate brows pleated and she hovered with perceptible uneasiness. Pink tinting her pale ivory skin, she dragged her attention from him only to be shaken by the compulsion to look afresh. It was as though a piece of indiscernible elastic were tightening and trying to jerk her eyes back to him again by force. 'I'm sorry—I don't understand. Look, I'll come back and finish this later.'

'No, do it now.' Sergio arrested her retreat in its tracks with the command. Her apparent bewilderment at his query was making him question his initial suspicions.

Arrogant, demanding, oversexed…Kathy gave him a rude label inside her head, a flush of angry embarrassment colouring her cheeks. She wanted out of his office: she wasn't stupid. She knew why he had asked if one of his friends had sent her. On another occasion a male member of staff had asked her hopefully if she was a strippergram girl. It infuriated her that such insulting assumptions should be made purely on the basis of her appearance. She was doing her job and she had the same right as anyone else to be left in peace to get on with it! As she knelt back down again she accidentally collided with black eyes that flared as golden as flames and momentarily held her transfixed. For a timeless moment she was still, breathing held in suspension, mouth running dry. Then she blinked, tore her attention free again with difficulty and discovered that her mind was a total blank, for his sensationally attractive image was now stamped there in place of rational thought.

Sergio was watching her every move and she made no effort that he could see to put on a show designed to draw his notice to her. Her clothing was unremarkable, the overall all-concealing. She was not provocative and her movements were very quiet, so why was he still watching her? There was something different about her, an unknown element that stood out and grabbed his attention. The pale pink blush of awareness that had swept her ivory complexion had sent his healthy male hormones on a rampant surge. Her amazing eyes were as green as the bitter-sweet apples his English grandfather had once grown and there was a surprisingly direct look in them. A lingering appraisal of the lush pout of her crushed strawberry mouth was sufficient to arouse him to a serious level of discomfort.

Kathy kept on working at the patch of carpet that she knew needed more specialist attention than she could give it. She was really fighting to think straight but she was amazed by her response to him. No man had had that effect on her since Gareth—and Gareth had never left her so bemused that she scarcely knew what she was doing. But then she had been in love, a dreaming teenager drifting along on a raft of foolish romantic expectations. Her reaction to the guy in the business suit, she reasoned feverishly, was just a reminder that Mother Nature had blessed her with the same physical chemistry as every other human being and sexual attraction was just a part of that. Maybe she should be welcoming the discovery that a broken heart and disillusionment hadn't entirely killed off her ability to feel like a normal woman.

'Excuse me…' she muttered with careful politeness, moving across the room to leave.

Instinct made Sergio spring upright. Near the doorway she lifted her bright head, her apple green eyes telegraphing her tension. The words of amused protest he had been about to voice to retain her presence went unspoken. *Madonna diavolo*, she was a cleaner and he a Torrente! His strong bone structure tautened, rigorous self-discipline reinstated. What was he thinking of? But he still could not accept that it was a coincidence that such a strikingly beautiful woman should be working so close to his office and conveniently available at his first call. It was even more unusual for him to work late without his customary support staff in attendance. It *had* to be some kind of a set-up!

Sergio was well aware that his fabulous wealth made him a constant target. Women frequently went to extreme lengths to catch his eye. Vital pieces of clothing slipped so that he could see what was on offer and how easily available it was. Any shade of gallantry in his character had turned to hardened cynicism while he was still a teenager. Too many maidens in distress had vied for his attention with fake incidents that ranged from cars that had broken down, doors that wouldn't unlock and flights that had been

mysteriously missed to last-minute accommodation problems and sudden attacks of illness. Innumerable women
had used the tactics of guile and trickery just to get the
chance to meet Sergio and spark his interest. A seemingly
respectable and very bright PA had once stripped down to
her saucy lingerie to bring him coffee, while several others
had used late meetings and business trips to get naked and
raunchy for his benefit. At the age of thirty-one, he had received countless sexual invitations, some subtle, most of
them bold and a few downright strange.

The door safely shut behind her again, Kathy drank in a
quivering breath of oxygen to replenish her starved lungs.
She wondered who he was and then discarded the thought
again. What did it matter to her who he was? On the way past
the chessboard, with its pieces fashioned of polished metal
and glittering stones, she hesitated, studied the state of play
and swiftly sacrificed a pawn, hoping to tempt the other
player into relaxing their guard. Was it *him*? She thought it
highly improbable: there were two other large offices linked
to that inner hallway and one of them contained half a dozen
desks. A posh guy with gold cuff links and a cold upper-class
accent that just shrieked an English public school education
struck her as a very unlikely candidate for exchanging long-
distance chess moves with a total stranger. She sped back
down the corridor to continue the work he had interrupted.

Sergio was closing his laptop when the phone rang.

'We've got the mysterious chess joker on camera, sir,'
Renzo revealed with satisfaction.

'When did you manage that? This evening?'

'The incident took place last night. I've had a man
checking the surveillance footage for hours. I think you'll
be surprised by what I've found out.'

'So, surprise me,' Sergio urged, stifling his impatience.

'It's a young woman, one of the maintenance staff, who works nights—a cleaner called Kathy Galvin. She started here a month ago.'

Incredulity awakened in Sergio's cool dark features and was swiftly followed by strong curiosity. 'Send the relevant images to my computer.'

Sergio ran the footage on screen while keeping Renzo on the telephone, and there she was: the ravishing redhead. He watched her get up from the sofa in the vestibule where she had evidently been taking a nap and stretch. With a cursory glance down at the board she moved the white knight. Was it sexist to suspect that someone much cleverer was advising her by mobile phone on her skilful game? She then began to tidy her tousled hair, unclasping it and pulling out a comb. He was put in mind of a mermaid showing off her crowning glory to tempt sailors onto the rocks. He wondered if she knew the camera was there while he feasted his attention on her exquisite face and froze her image on screen.

'It's misconduct, sir,' Renzo told him eagerly.

'You think so?' Sergio got up from his desk, taking the portable phone with him as he strolled out to take a look at the chessboard. Evidently she had abandoned caution and made another move directly after leaving his office. Why? No doubt she was keen to help him to speedily unveil her identity and take the bait. Illicit napping on the job aside, the humble toil of cleaning duties had to be a serious challenge for a woman only doing it in an effort to cross his path.

'She'll be disciplined, probably sacked by the contract company when we lodge a complaint—'

'No. Leave this matter with me and be discreet about it,' Sergio interposed softly. 'I'll handle it.'

'You'll handle it, sir?' his security chief repeated in audible astonishment. 'Are you sure?'

'Of course. I also want that surveillance camera put out of commission right now.' Sergio tossed the phone down. His astute dark eyes were shot through with derisive gold. So she wasn't a genuine hard-working salt-of-the-earth cleaner worthy of his respect. Why had he been willing to believe she was for even five minutes? Put that glorious face and body in tandem with the creative chess game aimed at attracting his attention and he had yet another gold-digger in hot and original pursuit.

Open season for the hunt, Sergio mused with sardonic amusement. He was a hell of a good shot and he intended to have some fun. And sooner rather than later, because he was leaving London the next day to compete in a cross-country skiing marathon in Norway. After that he had business to attend to in New York. It would be ten days before he was back in the UK.

Rising to his full imposing height of six feet three inches, Sergio strode out of the office and down the corridor in search of his quarry. He found her dusting a desk. Her fabulous hair glittered in multi-shaded splendour below the ceiling lights. When she straightened and saw him in the doorway, an expression of surprise grew on her delicate features. Grudging amusement assailed Sergio: she knew how to stay in role all right. Looking at that frowning air of enquiry, nobody would have dreamt that she had been teasing and tantalising him with a game that he considered very much his own for almost three weeks.

'Let's play chess in the real world, *bella mia*,' Sergio

suggested with silken cool. 'I challenge you to finish the game tonight. If you win, you get me. If you lose, you still get me. How can you lose?'

CHAPTER TWO

KATHY stared at Sergio Torrente for a good ten seconds. Her every expectation was shattered by that challenge coming at her out of the blue, and from such a source as the powerfully built male confronting her. For a long time now, she had protected herself by never taking a risk and never stepping out of line to be noticed. Sudden unexpected attention from a stranger and the belated realisation that she had foolishly invited it unnerved her.

Yet she was mortifyingly aware that it was his bold, dark masculine beauty that claimed her attention first. Win or lose, he was on offer? Was he serious? If he was, would she dare to take him up on it? While she'd worked she had told herself that he could not have been half as attractive as she had thought he was. Now here he was again in the flesh to blow that staid and sensible belief right out of the water. Just looking at the proud, chiselled planes of his darkly handsome features gave her the strangest sense of pleasure. A frisson of dangerous exhilaration gripped her while butterflies fluttered in her stomach. She parted her lips without even knowing what she intended to say. 'I—er—'

Glittering black eyes centred on her with laser beam intensity. 'Backing down from a face-to-face contest?' he murmured with unconcealed scorn.

Anger shot through Kathy with a power and sharpness that she had forgotten she could feel and she lifted her chin in answer. 'Are you kidding?'

Sergio stepped back to allow her to precede him from the room. 'Then let's go and play.'

'But I'm working,' Kathy pointed out with a slow bemused shake of her head. 'For goodness' sake, who are you?'

A mocking ebony brow quirked. 'Is that a serious question?'

'Why wouldn't it be?'

'I am Sergio Torrente and I own the Torrenco Group,' Sergio delivered drily, wondering whether she thought it was clever to make what he considered to be an outrageous claim of ignorance. 'Every company in this block belongs to me. I find it hard to believe that you're not aware of those facts.'

Kathy was paralysed to the spot by that revelation. It had not even occurred to her that he might be that important. But, even so, she had never heard of him before. She had never been on any floor other than the one she was on now and she had had no interest whatsoever in the business world or the personalities that powered the huge building during the hours of daylight.

'So will you play?' Sergio prompted with impatience.

An adrenalin rush was firing self-preservation skills in Kathy. It was clear to her that she had picked the wrong chessboard to get familiar with and the wrong guy. Why had she not even suspected that he might be her opponent? His smooth urbane façade had deceived her, she conceded tautly. He radiated an aura of sophisticated ease and cool.

But the breathtaking elegance of his designer suit concealed a purebred predator, for he was a highly aggressive and clever player who took advantage of every tactical opportunity to attack. In short, he was very much an Alpha male incapable of ignoring any perceived challenge to prove his strength. Not a guy to tangle with, not a guy to offend.

'I could take my break now,' Kathy told him, ready to get her punishment over with, as instead of beating him in two moves as she had previously planned she decided that it would be wiser to let him win.

Sergio nodded, hooded dark golden eyes nailed to her because he had yet to work out what script she was trying to follow. Was he really supposed to credit that she didn't know who he was?

'I've had the board moved into my office so that we can play undisturbed.'

Her heart was now beating very fast with nervous tension. He thrust open the door of his office, then stood back. Momentarily she was close enough to catch the faint evocative scent of some expensive male cologne. She snatched in a charged breath. 'How did you know it was me? How did you find out?'

'That's not important.'

'It's important to me,' she dared.

'Surveillance camera,' he supplied.

Kathy lost colour. There was a security camera in that hallway? She was appalled by that news. She took her breaks there and, once or twice, when she had been very tired, she had set the alarm on her watch and taken a nap on that sofa. Proof of those facts would be sufficient to put her out of a job.

'Would you like a drink?'

Her slender figure now tense as a bowstring, Kathy hovered in the centre of the carpet. A pool of light shone across the board and the sofas in one corner. It was a very intimate backdrop. If the supervisor came looking for her and found her in such a situation she would get totally the wrong idea and alcohol was a sackable offence. 'Are you trying to get me fired?'

'If you don't talk, I won't,' Sergio countered with lazy indifference.

An automatic negative was on Kathy's lips, but suddenly a spirit of rebellion sparked inside her. With the proof he already had of her stealing a nap during her break, there was little point splitting hairs. 'You're only young once,' Bridget had scolded that same day. But Kathy had never really known what it was to be young and carefree. Since she had regained her freedom she had followed every rule she met everywhere to the letter, no matter how small the rule, no matter how petty. The habit had become engrained in her, the new secure framework by which she lived. The chess game had been the only deviation and only because she couldn't resist the temptation of reliving the challenges her late father had once set her. In truth she could not even recall when she had last tasted alcohol and that made her feel pathetic, sad and defiant. She named a fashionable drink that she had seen advertised on a billboard.

'You seem very tense.' Sergio passed her a glass. Translucent green eyes rested on him, providing an alluring contrast to her alabaster skin and copper and red streaked hair. Predictably, he went straight for it. 'Don't stress, *bella mia*. I find you incredibly attractive.'

The annoyance and embarrassment that Kathy usually felt at such moments was entirely absent. So, he had been serious. She felt as if her heart were pounding right at the foot of her throat. She was shaken by the discovery that she was thrilled by his approach. Her fingers tightened round the glass, her hand shook a little. She sipped and swallowed, sipped and swallowed again, to conceal the reality of her physical weakness. It was so uncool to be so excited. Locked into his stunning dark golden gaze when she finally raised the courage to look up, she could not have breathed to save her life.

Unhurriedly, Sergio angled his lustrous dark head down. He was testing the boundaries, amusing himself. The delicate fresh scent of her skin made his strong, hard body tauten. Arousal slivered through him with a force that surprised him and speedily tipped him out of teasing mode. He claimed her luscious pink lips with hungry urgency and that first taste only whet his appetite for more.

Kathy couldn't credit what she was doing, but she wouldn't have shifted an inch to prevent it happening, either. A storm tide of feeling engulfed her and she couldn't get enough of it. It was as energising as hitching a ride on a rocket and it left her equally dizzy and disorientated. He kissed her and fireworks of sensation shot through her and she pulsed and tingled with response. Honeyed warmth pooled in her tummy, a tightness forming at her pelvis. She shivered violently when the sensual glide of his tongue probed the tender cave of her mouth. The throb of desire that flashed and stabbed through her slim length was almost too much to bear and she moaned in protest.

'You are so hot, you burn,' Sergio framed and, as his deep, dark drawl roughened, a faint Italian accent broke through to mellow the syllables with a lyrical edge. 'But we have a game to finish.'

Kathy wasn't quite sure her legs would keep her upright long enough to reach the sofa at her side of the board. She would have found it easier to fall back into his arms than walk away, an acknowledgement that shook her up even more. Her body felt tight, overheated and unfamiliar. She was aware of it in ways that were new to her. All the time her brain was set on enumerating her mistakes. She shouldn't be in a room alone with him, shouldn't have allowed him to kiss her, and certainly shouldn't have encouraged him by responding. But while her intelligence knew each and every one of those things, the hunger he had awakened and the dissatisfaction he had left behind had an even stronger hold on her.

Two moves later, the chess game was over.

When Sergio won, his black brows drew together and then anger illuminated his narrowed gaze to gilded bronze. 'Either someone else has been telling you how to play for the past three weeks, or you just deliberately threw the game to let me win!'

Kathy was dismayed by his discernment but determined to tough it out. 'You won…okay?'

'No, it is not okay. Which was it?' Sergio countered icily.

The silence felt suffocating. Tension made it hard for her to swallow. She scrambled up. 'I should get back to work.'

Hauteur stamped on his lean hard features, Sergio vaulted upright, well over six feet of lean, muscular male. 'You will go nowhere until you give me an answer.'

Kathy dealt him a troubled glance and screened her green eyes. His cold anger took her aback. 'My goodness, it's only a game,' she mumbled.

'Answer me,' Sergio commanded.

Kathy heaved a sigh and shifted her hands in a dismissive gesture. 'I let you win…all right?'

Sergio could not recall when he had last been so outraged by a woman. 'Is that what you believe I wanted or expected from you? Do you think I am so vain that I need a fake victory to bolster my ego?' he shot at her with stinging contempt. 'I don't need that kind of sacrifice and I don't like flattery. This is not the way to please me.'

Temper like a red-hot flame was darting through Kathy's willowy form. 'Well, then, you should stop throwing your weight around and behaving like a bully!' she launched back at him half an octave higher. 'How do you expect me to behave? How am I supposed to cope with you? Let's not pretend that this is a level playing field or that you gave me a choice—'

'Don't shout at me,' Sergio breathed glacially while inside he reeled in stunned disbelief from that condemnation.

'You wouldn't be listening otherwise. I'm sorry I touched your stupid chess set, but it was only meant to be a harmless piece of fun. I'm sorry I let you win and offended you. But I wasn't trying to please you—I couldn't care less about pleasing you!' Kathy flung back at him in disgust. 'I was trying to *placate* you…I'm supposed to be working. I don't want to lose my job. Can I get back to work now?'

Her attitude shone a bright revisionist light on the confrontation for Sergio. He had a brilliant penetrating mind and an unequalled talent for strategy. In business he was invincible, for he united the survival skills and killing instincts of a shark with a similar lack of emotion. He had learned early not to accept people at face value. But would a woman out to impress him shout at him? He had no evidence of anything calculated in Kathy Galvin's behaviour. Why should she have known who he was?

Sergio reached a decision on the basis of the facts. 'You really are just the cleaner.'

An affronted flush coloured Kathy's face as she wondered what on earth that comment was supposed to mean. Had he perhaps thought she was an undercover spy? Or a hooker moonlighting with a mop? 'Yes,' she said tightly. 'Just the cleaner—excuse me.'

As the door flipped shut on her quick exit Sergio swore softly in Italian, because he had not intended to humiliate her. The phone rang.

It was Renzo again. 'I've been running a check on the cleaning lady with the chess fetish—'

'Unnecessary,' Sergio interposed.

The older man cleared his throat. 'Galvin has a dodgy CV, sir. I don't think she's what she says she is. Although she's a very bright girl with a fistful of top grades from school, her employment record only contains some very recent restaurant work. It doesn't add up. There's a gap of three years and no adequate explanation for it. According to the résumé she was travelling all that time, but I don't buy it.'

'Neither do I.' His lean, strong face hard, Sergio considered the fact that for the first time in a decade he had almost been conned by a woman.

'I think she's probably another bimbo on the make, or even a paparazzo. I'll ask the cleaning company to remove her from the rota. Thankfully, she's their problem, not ours.'

But Sergio was unwilling to let Kathy Galvin off so easily. When had he ever walked away from a challenge?

Kathy worked at speed in an attempt to lose her troubled thoughts in energetic activity. The treatment she had received had left her angry and bewildered. Sergio Torrente was a gorgeous guy with an attitude problem. A rampant snob and very proud. Cool at best, he was colder than ice when he was crossed. But when he had kissed her, pure naked excitement had made mincemeat of all his faults. Had he momentarily contrived to forget that she was *just* the cleaner? He must have done. He was probably at least thirty years old and way too mature for her. She rammed the mop into the bucket with noisy unnecessary force. She had nothing in common with some super-rich older guy who owned a building and made a big fuss when some lesser mortal dared to muck around with his chessboard!

She began to wonder if she was fated to die a virgin. Year after year, life was steadily passing her by. Sergio Torrente was the first bloke she had fancied since Gareth had dumped her. How clever was that? Sexual chemistry was very strange, she mused ruefully. Why hadn't she warmed to one of the many men who had tried to chat her up at the café? Obviously she was being rather too fussy. Even so, she was convinced that nine out of ten women would find Sergio Torrente pretty much irresistible. She had never gone for boyish men or the type who might almost be described as pretty. His lean dark features contrived to unite classic good looks with a raw and compelling masculinity that was seriously sexy, Kathy ruminated dreamily, wielding her mop with less and less vigour.

'Kathy…?'

Her head flew up, light green eyes preoccupied. When she saw the subject of her most intimate thoughts standing just ten feet from her she did a double take. As she felt her wretched skin colouring up in a wave of guilty heat she wanted the ground to open up and swallow her alive. 'Yes?'

'I owe you an apology.'

Kathy nodded in firm agreement.

Sergio, who had been awaiting a flattering protest at that statement, laughed with reluctant appreciation. She was turning in a prize-winning performance in the sincerity stakes. Was her candour supposed to strike him as a refreshing quality? Appeal to his jaded billionaire palate and need for novelty? He didn't know and he didn't care. The fawn-like lashes swept down on her amazing eyes and desire dug talon claws of need into his groin. What did it matter if she sold her story afterwards to some tacky tabloid? One glimpse of her exquisite face and the most basic of male instincts took over. His reaction to her was atavistic and stronger than anything he had felt in a long time. To look at her without touching her almost hurt. He knew that the only thing that would satisfy him now was bedding her. He had never been into self-denial.

'Will you play another game with me when your shift ends?' Sergio asked silkily.

Kathy was astonished by the apology and the renewed invitation. In a wary and fleeting collision with brilliant dark eyes as crystal-clear and cold as an underground lake, she sensed the danger of him: the powerful personality reined in below the surface. Clever, ruthless, definitely not the sort of male anyone would want as an enemy. It dismayed her that even sensing those hard-nosed qualities she should still find him incredibly attractive. She swallowed hard, struggling to pay heed to her misgivings. 'I'm afraid I don't finish until eleven o'clock.'

'It's not a problem.'

'No?' Temptation was tugging at her with relentless force.

'No. I haven't eaten yet. I'll send a car to pick you up when you're finished.'

'Can't we just play here?' Kathy gave way but only on terms that she felt would be comfortable for her. She didn't want to risk being seen with him. Nor did she want to climb into some strange car to be taken heaven knew where and possibly left to find her own way home again in the early hours of the morning.

His surprise was patent. 'If that's what you want.'

'It is.'

Kathy watched his long fluid stride carry him out of her sight. She was in a daze, not quite able to accept that he had talked her round with very little effort. It was only a game of chess, she told herself in sudden exasperation. He was still set on winning. If he kissed her again, she would…well, she would just make sure that they didn't get that close. It would be pointless, him with his business empire and her with her history. And she didn't want to be kicked in the teeth again, did she? There was no point literally queuing up to get hurt. But nor was there any harm in pitting her wits against his.

Five minutes before eleven, Kathy freshened up in the cloakroom. She folded up her overall and dug it into her bag. Her turquoise cotton T-shirt clung to her minimal curves. She turned sideways, breathed in deep and arched her spine. Her bosom remained disappointingly slight from every angle. Meeting her own eyes in the mirror, she flushed in embarrassment and concentrated on brushing her hair instead.

Kathy was twenty-three years old but, just then, she felt more like a nervous teenager. That lowering feeling of ignorance and insecurity annoyed her. The years between nineteen and twenty-two, when she might have acquired a little more experience, had been stolen from her. As soon as that bitter thought occurred to her, she buried it again, for she tried never to look back in that spirit; it did her no good to dwell on what could not be changed. She had spent three years in prison for a crime she had not committed and still bore the scars, mentally and physically. But few had been willing to believe in her innocence and indeed had often judged her more harshly for daring to make such a claim. Get over it, she told herself firmly; leave it in the past, move on.

When she walked into his office, her lissom figure and endless long coltish legs merely enhanced by a T-shirt and jeans, Sergio was startled by her impact. The exotic slant of her cheekbones was more obvious with her glorious hair tumbling in loose waves round her narrow shoulders— hair the colour of tangerine marmalade in sunlight, glinting with amber and ochre shades that acted as a superb showcase for her white skin and apple-green eyes.

'Have you ever been a model?' he asked while he poured her another drink.

'No. I don't fancy walking half naked down a catwalk. I like food too much, as well. Could you spare a packet of crisps?' Her tummy grumbling with hunger, Kathy had noticed the snacks in the snazzy drinks cabinet that stood open.

'Help yourself. You seem more relaxed than you were earlier,' Sergio remarked.

'I'm on my own free time.' Kathy curled up on the sofa and munched crisps while she played. The salty snack made her thirsty and she had to keep on sipping her drink. She only allowed herself to study him closely several moves into the game when he seemed unaware of her attention.

But no matter how much she looked at him, Sergio

Torrente still took her breath away. He was drop-dead beautiful. Hair and lashes with the sheen of black silk, mesmeric dark eyes, a strong sensual mouth. He had shaved since she had last seen him—the faint bluish shadow of stubble had vanished. She wondered if that meant he planned to kiss her again. Heat pooled in her tummy and warmed more intimate places with a physical awareness that took her aback. She reminded herself that she had come to play chess, not to flirt.

Sergio glanced up. 'Your move.'

Her lashes dropping in a protective screen over her eyes, she studied the board.

Sergio watched her demonstrate a skill, speed and assurance that made it clear that she was well able to hold her own. 'Who taught you to play?'

'My father.'

'So did mine.' His lean strong face shadowed. Silence lay before he matched her on the board and then, noticing her empty glass, he rose to refill it.

Her light green eyes rested on him throughout the exercise. Everything about him fascinated her: the classy cut of his hair, the designer *élan* of his suit, the discreet gleam of gold at his wrist and cuff, the fluid way he moved his lean brown hands when he spoke. He was very elegant and very controlled.

'If you keep on looking at me like that, we'll never finish the game, *bella mia*.'

Kathy reddened and took the glass he extended with a hand that wasn't quite steady. He had read her so easily it embarrassed her. It also reminded her of how little she knew about him. As she thought of what she should have asked at the outset she tensed. 'Are you married?'

Surprise made Sergio quirk an ebony brow. 'Why are you asking?'

'Is that a yes or a no?'

'I'm single.'

Although her head was swimming a little, Kathy side-stepped the trap he had set for her on the board and shot him a victorious smile.

'You're good,' Sergio conceded, amused by the suspicion that she too might have set out to play a very fast game. 'We have a tie. Tact or fact?'

'Fact.'

Her cheeky grin of challenge brought out the caveman in him.

He leant down, closed a hand into her tumbling copper-streaked tresses to raise her face to his and drove her delectable pink lips hungrily apart, making love to her mouth with devastating expertise.

That sudden taste of him took Kathy by storm. Desire exploded through her slender length like a depth charge that ignited on impact. Shards of sensation rippled through her. He kissed with an eroticism that was spellbinding. As he pulled her up against him her arms went round him to steady herself because she was dizzy. The alcohol? She shut down that suspicion, suddenly determined not to succumb to her need to play safe again. She was breathless with excitement, her heart pounding like mad. For the first time that she could remember she felt young and fearless and alive.

'I can't keep my hands off you,' Sergio told her softly.

'We were playing chess,' Kathy reminded him in a breathless whisper.

'I want to play with you instead, *delizia mia*.'

That was a touch too blunt for her. Her cheeks flamed, her confusion patent. With a sardonic laugh, he raked smouldering golden eyes over her exquisite face. He lowered his handsome dark head again. The invasive stab of his tongue inside her mouth was deliciously sensual and she pressed helplessly closer to his hard masculine frame for more. Against her lower stomach she could feel the hard, intimate proof of his arousal and she shivered. Her hands fixed to the wide, steely strength of his shoulders. Her response overwhelmed and ensnared her. A tight little knot of desire was unfurling low in her pelvis, filling her with yearning and impatience. Even her senses seemed to have gone into hyperactive mode: her fingers filtered through his springy black hair and rejoiced in the silken texture while the already familiar scent of his skin acted on her like an aphrodisiac.

Sergio had planned to finish the game first and it had finished on schedule. Sergio always planned everything. But desire was a raging fire in his blood and that driving intensity was novel to him. Her slim body slotted into his lean powerful frame as though she had been born to make that connection. What he was feeling was addictive and he wanted more of it and *all* of her. He lowered her down on the sofa and discarded his jacket and tie.

That temporary separation made Kathy tense and question what she was doing. Even though her mind was fuzzy, she told herself to get up. Hair spread in a burnished mass of Titian splendour round her head, she looked up at him, eyes glazed with passion and uncertainty, her generous mouth rosy red from the attention of his. He chose that particular moment to smile down at her. 'You are gorgeous,' he told her and it was a smile of such charismatic power that she felt as though her heart were bouncing like a rubber ball inside her chest.

A tiny pulse was going crazy at her collar-bone. Sergio put his mouth to the delicate blue-veined skin and she gasped and arrowed up to him. Her body was thrumming like an engine that was raring to go and she didn't know how to handle the stress of it. He found the bare skin below her T-shirt and closed his hand to a tiny, sweet pouting mound. For an instant she went stiff because she had forgotten that she had no bra on and there was no warning before he found the part of her body that she was least confident about. He pushed the turquoise fabric out of his path and exposed her small breasts to his appreciative scrutiny.

'Ravishing,' Sergio pronounced with satisfaction, catching a pouting nipple the colour of a tea rose between thumb and finger and chafing the delicate bud until a smothered sound of response was wrenched from her. He used his tongue to moisten the distended crest and it was only the beginning of a slow process of sensual torment. Her hips jerked and shifted with increasing frequency, her thighs pressing together on the ache of emptiness that was stirring between them. Her breath rasped in her throat as he toyed with the sensitised nubs until they were stiff and taut and wildly responsive to his every caress.

Reaction was piling onto reaction too fast for her to bear. She was on the heights of a frantic anticipation that utterly controlled her. He coiled back from her to peel off her jeans. For an instant awareness returned to her when she rocked back up into sitting position to blink in vague surprise at the sight of her bare legs. Tiny tremors of frantic desire were quivering through her. She met hot golden eyes and burned inside and out, sensible thought sizzling into nothingness.

'Sergio,' she whispered wonderingly.

That fast he recaptured her attention. He meshed long brown fingers into the vibrant fall of her hair and kissed her with devouring passion. She resented the distraction when something caught in her hair and pulled it hard enough to make her mutter in complaint.

'Be still. Your hair's caught,' he groaned, unclasping his designer watch to disentangle her from the bracelet and removing the timepiece to toss it aside.

Kathy struggled with the buttons on his shirt until he leant back and wrenched it off for her. 'You need practice,' he told her thickly. 'I'll give you all you can handle, *delizia mia.*'

The hair-roughened contours of his warm muscular torso felt amazing beneath her palms. She wanted to explore further, but he pushed her back against the arm of the sofa to take her mouth with ravenous need. At the same instant that he discovered the moist, swollen heart of her, conscious choices evaporated for her. She had never been touched there before and never dreamt that she could be quite so sensitive. But he had the erotic skill to show her. Exquisite sensation engulfed her in mindless pleasure and she shivered and writhed and whimpered.

Sergio had never been so aroused by a woman. There was no thought now of who she was or what she might be. Her passionate out-of-control response exploded his customary cool like dynamite. Once his powerful sensuality was unleashed, he was all decisive action. He came over her in one slick movement. She trembled, suddenly aware of the feel of his hot, probing intrusion in that most tender place. Her eyes widened and she tensed in disquiet at virtually the same moment as he entered her with an earthy groan of satisfaction. She was unprepared for the sharp stab of pure piercing pain that provoked a cry of dismay from her lips before she could bite it back.

Ebony brows pleating, Sergio stared down at her with frowning golden eyes of enquiry. '*Per meraviglia*…I am the first?'

'Don't stop.' Kathy shut her eyes tight. It was like being in the grip of a whirlwind, for even as the pangs of pain receded her body still signalled a powerful craving for the urgency of his.

He sank his hands below her hips to ease his passage with a slow sexual skill that was breathtakingly erotic. Her heart hammered as he taught her his sensual masculine rhythm with a boldness that delighted her senses. The excitement flooded back even stronger than before. Ripples of pleasure began to build, gripping her tighter and tighter in a torment of need she could not withstand. She reached for the ultimate and shattered in a climax that consumed her at hurricane force and plunged her into a free fall of delight.

The delight was short-lived.

Sergio held her close. 'It's a long time since any woman made me feel so good, *bellezza mia*,' he murmured raggedly.

Kathy was still shell-shocked by the entire experience and revelling in a sense of physical connection that was seductively new to her. 'I've never felt like this…ever,' she added helplessly.

'I have one vital question.' Sergio stared down at her with disturbingly cool and assessing dark eyes. 'Why did you give me your virginity?'

Kathy was dismayed by that direct question, particularly as he was suggesting that she had made some kind of a decision while she was all too uneasily aware that she had been considerably less mature in the nature of her giving.

Taut with suspicion of her motives, Sergio shook his handsome dark head. 'It was a very gratifying experience and not one I ever expected to have,' he confided flatly. 'But I know and I accept that any special pleasure always comes at a cost and I would really prefer to know right now up front what you want in return.'

Her smooth brow furrowed. 'Why should it cost you anything?'

'I'm a very rich man. I can't recall when I last enjoyed a freebie,' Sergio countered with sibilant derision.

When Kathy finally grasped his meaning she was appalled. She snaked her slim body free of his weight in an irate gesture of repudiation. How could she have shared her body with a guy who seemed to think that she would want to reap a financial reward from the activity? She could not have felt more ashamed had she been forced to walk down a street naked with the word *whore* written on a placard and hung round her neck.

Forced back from her by her sudden unanticipated retreat, Sergio had discovered another even more immediate source for concern. He cursed under his breath in Italian. 'Are you using birth control? In any form?'

Kathy was feeling dizzy and sick and distraught. She could not credit what she had done. She could not credit how stupid she had been. But while she was still in his presence she would not allow herself to think about those realities. All her energy was now concentrated on beating a very fast retreat from the scene of her worst ever mistake. She reached for her clothing. 'No—but you used contraception.'

Lean dark features uniformly grim, Sergio was getting dressed. 'The condom tore.'

Kathy flinched and turned paler than ever but she said

nothing in response. Indeed she refused even to look at him. This is what it's like when you get intimate with someone you don't know—awkward, humiliating, shaming, she reflected painfully. She fought her way into her panties with trembling hands, hauled on her T-shirt and wrenched on her jeans with so much force that she scratched the skin on her thighs.

'Obviously that doesn't bother you too much,' Sergio growled, outraged that she was simply ignoring him.

'What bothers me most at this moment is that I had sex with a truly horrible guy. I know I'm going to live with this mistake for a long, long time,' Kathy shared in a low-pitched tone of fierce regret. 'Getting pregnant by you would add a whole new dimension to this nightmare and I can't believe that even I could be that unlucky.'

'I doubt if that will be your reaction if it happens. Having my child could be a very lucrative lifestyle choice,' Sergio drawled with icy bite.

'Why do you think everyone's out to rip you off?' Kathy demanded in the rage that was steadily banishing any desire she might have had to take refuge in a small dark corner. 'Or is it just me you reserve the offensive accusations for? You really shouldn't mess around with the cleaning staff, Mr Torrente. Your nerves aren't cut out for it!'

'You need to calm down so that we can discuss this like adults.' Sergio breathed, glittering dark eyes locking to her with determined force, his expectations once again turned upside down by her behaviour. 'Sit down, please.'

'No.' Kathy shook her head vehemently, her wildly tousled copper-streaked hair flying back from her flushed cheekbones in vibrant splendour. 'I don't want to discuss anything with you. I had too much to drink. I did something I wish I hadn't done. You have been very, very rude to me.'

'That was not my intention.' Sergio aimed at striking a peaceful note, while he continued to watch her with shrewd concentration. Her heated distress was convincingly real and she was definitely slurring her words a little. She looked very young and quite magnificent.

Kathy loosed an unimpressed laugh, for she was not taken in by that smooth inflection. 'No, you couldn't care less if you were rude or not! You think you can get away with it.'

'You could well be right,' Sergio drawled in the same even tone. 'It's an unfortunate fact that gold-diggers target me—'

'You *deserve* a gold-digger!' Kathy snapped with furious conviction. 'If you think for one minute that that explanation excuses you for talking to me as if I was a prostitute, you're seriously out of line!'

'I wasn't aware that I made an excuse.'

Scornful dismissal flamed in Kathy's shimmering gaze. 'You haven't even got the manners for that, have you?'

'If you could rise above my failings in that department, I believe we have more important things to consider—'

'I doubt if I'll be pregnant, but if the worst was to happen, you don't need to worry,' Kathy tossed at him glibly as she walked to the door. 'I wouldn't even consider going for the "lucrative lifestyle choice" option!'

'That's not funny,' Sergio intoned grimly.

'Neither are your assumptions about me.' Kathy marched down the corridor, and when she registered that he was following her she hastened into the lift at speed. There she stabbed repeatedly at the button that closed the doors but he still made it past them to join her. The enclosed space felt unbearably claustrophobic. Hostility radiating from her in waves, her willowy figure rigid, she ignored him. She could not understand why he refused to get the message and leave her alone.

Sergio glanced down at his watch only to discover that he was no longer wearing it: he had left his sleek timepiece behind in his office. 'It's late. I'll take you home.'

'No, thanks.'

As the lift came to a halt Sergio imposed his lean powerful frame between her and the doors opening. 'I'll take you home,' he told her steadily.

'What is it about the word *no* that you don't understand?'

Sergio shifted closer. His intent dark gaze flared gold over her mutinous face. Her continuing defiance and refusal to be reasonable was so far outside his usual experience with women that he was astonished.

'You're in my way. I'm getting annoyed with you,' Kathy warned him, an unevenly drawn breath rasping in her throat as she fired an unwilling glance at him. His dark gaze flashed down into hers like a livewire connection. Excitement came at her out of nowhere. Her heartbeat broke into a sprint, her mouth ran dry.

'But you feel the burn between us the same way I do, *bella mia*,' Sergio husked, reaching out to frame her cheekbones between shapely brown hands, his thumbs delicately smoothing over her fine creamy skin.

For the merest instant she was frozen there, tantalised by his approach and teased by his touch. She was extraordinarily aware of the intimate ache between her thighs and his intense sexual magnetism. Her brain had no control over her body. It terrified her that he could still win that response from her and angry defensiveness overcame her paralysis and forced her into urgent denial. 'I don't feel anything!'

Sidestepping him in an impulsive move that took him by surprise, Kathy stalked across the brightly lit empty space of the vast foyer and headed straight for the exit doors. She was in total turmoil, deeply disturbed by what she had allowed to happen between them.

'Kathy,' Sergio grated, his patience on the ebb since he had not believed that she would actually walk away from him.

'Get lost!' Kathy told him roundly, impervious to the fact that they had an audience. One of the two night security guards on duty, both of whom had been studiously staring into space, abruptly unfroze to hurry forward and thrust a door wide for her. She walked out onto the street.

Renzo Catallone moved forward from his discreet position in the shadow of a pillar to intercept his employer. A stocky man in his forties, he looked unusually ill at ease. 'I—'

'While I appreciate that it is your job to take care of my security, your zeal is occasionally more than I require,' Sergio informed his security chief drily. 'No more enquiries or checks on Kathy Galvin. She's off limits.'

'But—sir—' Renzo began with a frown of dismay.

'I don't want to hear another word about her,' Sergio instructed in a flat tone of finality. 'With the exception of one piece of information: the lady's address.'

CHAPTER THREE

KATHY LAY IN BED sleepless far into the night.

She tossed and turned, her emotions reeling between anger, hurt, shame and resentment. Above all she was disappointed in herself. Why hadn't she paid heed to her misgivings? Bored of the dullness of her life, she had rebelled like a headstrong teenager. She had lived too quietly, played too safe and Sergio Torrente had been more temptation than she could withstand. But she blamed the alcohol for making her reckless. Why had she pretended that the only attraction on offer was a game of chess?

She splayed apprehensive fingers across her concave tummy. The very idea of falling pregnant terrified her: taking care of her own needs was enough of a challenge. She told herself off for panicking. What was that going to achieve? Why did she always expect the worst? It was true that she had suffered some serious bad luck in recent years, but then, she reasoned doggedly, everybody had to live through bad times at some stage.

The next morning she fed Tigger and tried to think only resolutely upbeat thoughts. It was her day off and she could not afford to waste it. She needed to do research at the library for an essay. For the past year she had been studying for a degree with the Open University. On the way to the library, however, she called into a pharmacy and read the small print on the back of a pregnancy test to work out how soon she could use one.

She was queuing for the bus when her mobile phone rang. The cleaning company had received a complaint about her performance at the Torrenco building and, as a result, her services were no longer required.

Being sacked hit Kathy like a bolt from the blue. Sergio Torrente had had her fired! How could any guy sink that low? But, then, was such callous behaviour really that unusual? She suffered an unwelcome recollection of being dumped—not by Gareth but by his mother—and her tummy lurched in humiliated remembrance. Her childhood sweetheart had not even had the courage to tell her himself. He had abandoned her at a time when his support had felt like her only hope. His lack of faith in her had made her imprisonment for a crime she had not committed all the harder to bear.

Her memory dragged her back to the summer she had finished school. Her plans to study law at university had been on hold because her father was dying. After he had passed away, she'd had six months to fill before she could take up her deferred university place. She had accepted a live-in job as a career for Agnes Taplow, an elderly woman whom Kathy had been told was suffering from dementia.

When the old lady complained to Kathy that pieces of her antique silver collection were going missing, Agnes Taplow's niece had assured Kathy that her aunt was imagining things. But items had continued to disappear without trace. The police had been called in to investigate and a small but rare early Georgian jug had been found in

Kathy's handbag. That same day Kathy had been charged with theft. Initially she had been confident that the true culprit, who could only have hidden the jug in her bag to implicate her, would soon be exposed. Caught up in a web of deceit and lies, and with no family of her own to fight her corner, Kathy had been unable to prove her innocence. The court had found her guilty of theft and she'd had to serve her prison sentence.

But those events had taken place at a time when she was too immature and powerless to act in her own defence, Kathy reminded herself urgently. Since then she had learned how to look after herself. Why should she allow Sergio Torrente to get away with putting her out of work? It was hard to see how she could prevent him. He had wealth, status and power and she had none of those things. But even if she couldn't change anything she had the right to tell him what she thought of him. Indeed standing up for the sake of her self-esteem felt like the only strength she had left.

'I'm afraid there's no sign of your watch, Mr Torrente. I've searched every inch of your office,' the security man reported ruefully.

With a faint frown marking his sleek ebony brows, Sergio rose from behind his desk because he had a flight to Norway to catch. Of course there would be a simple explanation. When he had discarded his watch the night before, it must have fallen somewhere beneath the furniture. Searches were rarely as thorough as people liked to think they were. The watch was mislaid, rather than missing, and theft was an unlikely possibility. He did not suffer from Renzo's paranoia about strangers. It would, however,

Sergio felt, be naïve to overlook the fact that his platinum watch was extremely valuable.

His entire personal staff was engaged in an urgent whispered consultation by the door. He was exasperated by the cloud of stress and indecision that hung over them. His efficient senior executive assistant was on vacation and her subordinates seemed lost without her. Finally, one broke away from the group and approached him in an apologetic manner. 'A woman called Kathy Galvin is out in Reception, sir. She's not on the approved list but she seems convinced that you will want to see her.'

Cool, hard satisfaction stamped Sergio's darkly handsome face. As he had suspected, Kathy's big walk-out had been an empty gesture. He was relieved that he had not sent her flowers, for conciliatory gestures were not his style. 'I do. She can travel to the airport with me.'

The PA could not conceal his surprise, since Sergio never saw anyone without an appointment and the women in his life invariably knew better than to interrupt his working day. A pleasurable sense of sexual anticipation building, Sergio began to plan his return to London in a fortnight's time. He strolled out to the private lift that would whisk him down to the car park.

Her vibrant head held high, soft colour defining her slanting cheekbones and bright green eyes, Kathy stepped through the door that had been opened for her. Her heart was beating very fast. Having assumed she was being granted a private meeting with Sergio, she was dismayed when she saw him standing with other men in the corridor. Tall, broad shouldered and dark, he dominated the group in more than the physical sense as he had the potent presence of a powerful man.

As Kathy had no intention of telling Sergio Torrente what she thought of him in front of an audience she was forced to contain her temper. The effort required made her feel like a pressure-cooker on the boil. Nor was her anger soothed by the discovery that that lean, hard-boned face of his could still send a jolt of response through her that was the equivalent of an electric shock. Imperious dark eyes unreadable, he directed her into the lift ahead of him. A positive aristocrat of good breeding and manners, she labelled inwardly, her teeth gritting. She was not impressed by the surface show.

'I suppose your aim is to get me out of here with the minimum of fuss,' Kathy condemned hotly.

Sergio was still engaged in tracking his glittering gaze over her gorgeous face and the amazing lithe, long-legged perfection of her body. His companions had studied her like a row of gobsmacked schoolboys. A striking effect, he acknowledged, for a woman who wasn't wearing either make-up or designer clothes. 'No, I'm heading to the airport. You can keep me company on the journey.'

'Don't waste your time with the charm offensive. I can hardly stick being this close to you in a lift!' Kathy hissed back at him at the speed of a bullet. 'You complained about me and I've been sacked. I'm only here to tell you what I think of your despicable behaviour—'

The lift doors glided open again on an underground car park. 'I lodged no complaint.'

'Someone did. But I didn't damage your chess set and I always completed my work targets—'

'It is possible that the enquiries made about you by my security advisors may have been construed as a complaint,' Sergio conceded, striding out of the lift. 'Given the tempo-

rary nature of your contract, your employer may have decided
that dispensing with your services was the wisest option.'

Hurrying along by his side, Kathy didn't know whether
to believe that interpretation or not. 'If that's the case, then
you should play fair and sort it out for me.'

But Sergio had a different take on the situation. He was
not disappointed by the news that she would no longer be
cleaning the Torrenco building. He thought that was definitely
a development to be welcomed. If she was about to figure in
his life in any guise she could not be engaged in such lowly
work. 'I'll fix you up with something more appropriate—'

'I don't want you fixing me up with anything!' Kathy
was incredulous at that cool response. 'I'm not asking for
favours either, only fair treatment.'

'We'll discuss it in the limo,' Sergio intoned smoothly.

Disconcerted by that proposal, Kathy finally dragged
her attention from Sergio for long enough to notice her immediate surroundings. A uniformed chauffeur was holding
wide the passenger door of a huge gleaming limousine,
while several men with the build of professional bodyguards hovered in a protective circle. Extreme discomfiture assailed her; she felt out of her depth. Even so, she also
recognised that getting into the car with him was the price
of continuing the dialogue. She climbed in and tried hard
not to gawp at the opulent leather interior and the sleek
built-in bank of business and entertainment equipment.

'Naturally you're annoyed. It is most regrettable that
you should have suffered unjust treatment,' Sergio intoned.

The dark, deep timbre of his voice sent a sinuous little
frisson snaking down Kathy's spine. But it also crossed her
mind that he was clever enough to know exactly what to
say and how to say it on any given occasion. Distrust

slivered through her and she stiffened like a cat stroked the wrong way. 'I'm glad that you recognise that it was unfair.'

'You don't need to worry,' Sergio countered with supreme assurance. 'I'll ensure that you get another job. '

'Easier said than done. I've only got a good reference as a waitress.' Kathy was already planning to take on extra shifts at the café to make ends meet. But the cracking pace of waiting tables for longer hours would exhaust her and her studies would suffer, so that option would only be useful in the short term.

'Would you prefer to work in the catering trade?'

'No.' Kathy closed her hands together in a taut movement. Even though it was his fault that she was in a tight corner she had a lot of pride and found it very hard to ask anyone for help. But if he had the influence he seemed to think he had, there was a chance that just for once a piece of bad luck could be turned into something more positive. 'I would love an office job,' she confided in a rush. 'It doesn't matter how junior it is. Even a temporary position would do, because it would give me some experience. I've got good IT skills…and a rather empty CV.'

'It's not a problem. I own a chain of employment agencies. I'll organise it today.'

'I'm not asking for any special favours,' she said defensively.

'I'm not offering any.' Sergio closed a confident hand over hers, unfurling her taut white fingers to tug her closer.

Her green eyes were wary. 'Look, I'm not here for the seduction routine.'

'Your pulse says otherwise, *bella mia*,' Sergio traded huskily, his thumb and forefinger encircling her fragile wrist while he challenged her with smouldering dark golden eyes.

That single look was so hot that Kathy felt as though she were burning inside her skin. A lightning strike of desire slivered through her, stinging her nipples into straining needle points, creating a knot of tension in her pelvis. In a sudden compulsive movement that had nothing to do with thought she leant forward and found his shapely sensual mouth for herself. A split second later she could not believe that she had made the first move, but she could no more have resisted that primitive prompting than she could have stopped breathing.

His powerful libido ignited by that boldness, Sergio drove her soft pink lips apart with answering passion. He delved into the moist interior of her mouth with a rhythmic eroticism that drove her wild with longing. Her fingers raked through his gleaming black hair, holding him to her. One kiss only led to the next and the exchange was frantic, increasingly forceful and infuriatingly unsatisfying for both of them. With a groan of frustration he hauled her slim body closer, closing his hand over hers to guide it down to the furious power of his erection.

Her fingers spread over the swell of his male arousal, outrageously obvious even through the fabric of his trousers. Wanton damp heat flowered at the tender heart of her body and she quivered, shot through and weak with sheer longing and excitement. She knew what he wanted and she knew what she wanted to do, though it was something that had never before had the slightest appeal to her. The shock of that sexual intensity made her eyes fly open.

It was disconcerting to recognise that it was still broad daylight and that they were in a moving car in traffic. She had forgotten everything, where she was, who she was. She felt out of control and it scared her. Tearing her reddened mouth from his, she sucked in a steadying breath and shifted her hand onto his long powerful thigh.

A lean brown hand closed into her copper hair to stop her moving back out of reach. Scorching golden eyes held her fast. 'You shouldn't start anything you're not prepared to finish.'

'I've got work to do.' Kathy lifted her chin, her cheeks burning.

Accustomed to instant compliance with his wishes, Sergio studied her with shimmering dark eyes of hauteur. Then he flung his arrogant head back and vented an appreciative laugh. He liked her nerve. 'What work?'

'I have another part-time job. I'm also studying.'

'And I have a flight to catch.'

Her heart thudded heavily inside her ribcage. He ran a slow caressing forefinger across the swollen curve of her lower lip. Her nerve-endings prickled with awareness. It took all her self-discipline not to lean forward and invite a greater intimacy.

'I'll see you when I get back to London—in a couple of weeks, *delizia mia*,' Sergio murmured softly.

'A couple of weeks?' Kathy queried in bemusement.

He explained his schedule. Intense disappointment filled her that he would be abroad for so long. She veiled her eyes, irritated by her juvenile response, her previous doubts setting in again. What was the point of seeing him again? Did she have novelty value? Even if he was interested in her, it would only be for all of five minutes. She needed no great experience of men to know that all she had to offer on his terms was her face and body. Was that enough for her?

Sergio checked his watch, only to rediscover for the tenth

time that morning that it wasn't on his wrist. Fortunately a replacement awaited him at the airport. 'I took off my watch last night. Did you notice where I put it?'

Her smooth brow furrowed. 'It was lying on the carpet. I stepped over it. Look, us seeing each other again isn't a good idea—'

His dark stare was unnervingly direct. 'Try keeping me away.'

'I'm serious—'

Sergio lifted the phone and punched in a number. A moment later he was talking in rapid Italian.

'Would you be interested in becoming a receptionist?' he enquired in casual aside.

Kathy nodded in immediate eager acknowledgement. After a brief further dialogue he replaced the phone and gave her an address to go to the following morning. 'For an interview?' she asked.

'No, the job's yours for three months. Longer, if you make a good impression.'

'Thanks,' she muttered awkwardly as the limo came to a halt.

'I owed you.' Sergio stepped out.

Uncertainly Kathy climbed out, as well, but he didn't notice; he was already walking away with two of his bodyguards following close behind him. His departure was the epitome of casualness. Before she sank back into the limo, she noticed a stocky older man on the pavement treating her to a flinty appraisal. His gloomy face was vaguely familiar and she knew she had seen him before, even if she could not recall where. When he got into the car behind, which previously had disgorged the bodyguards, she realised that he must work for Sergio.

The chauffeur captured her attention by asking her where she wanted to go. As the luxury vehicle moved off again to drop her at the library, she was in a happy daze at the prospect of starting a new job.

Almost two weeks later, Sergio arrived back in London. He was in an excellent mood.

Grave-faced, Renzo Catallone met his employer off his private jet and passed him a slim file.

'I realise I'm putting my job on the line here. But I can't be in charge of your personal security and keep quiet,' the security chief declared tautly. 'It's vital that you take a look at this dossier. I'm convinced that your watch has been stolen.'

CHAPTER FOUR

EYES AS BRIGHT AS STARS, Kathy studied her reflection in the mirror.

'Put on a pair of sunglasses and a bored expression and you'll be taken for a celebrity!' Bridget Kirk teased, her cheerful face wreathed in smiles.

Kathy was dressed in a vintage sixties dress the zingy yellow of a citrus fruit. It was a sleeveless sheath that hugged her slight curves as though it had been custom-made, and Kathy thought it gave her an amazingly classy look. She felt that that was an important consideration for a date with a guy who had been born into a family with a history that stretched back several centuries. While she was by no means intimidated by Sergio Torrente's background, which she had checked out on the internet, she had cringed at the reality that he might well wince if she turned out to see him in another pair of jeans. In actuality her wardrobe contained nothing fancier than black trousers.

And trying to remedy that problem on her income in the first weeks of a new job was out of the question. The struggle to survive until she received her first pay as a receptionist was proving a major challenge, even though she had worked almost every night at the café. She was very lucky that Bridget had come to her rescue with the suggestion that she might borrow an outfit from the café manager's vintage fashion collection accumulated from various charity shops.

'I don't know how to thank you.' Kathy enveloped the older woman in an impulsive hug. 'I know how proud you are of your clothes and I promise I'll look after the dress.'

Delighted to see Kathy so animated and talkative, Bridget returned the hug with enthusiasm. 'I'm pleased that you're finally going out on a date!'

'But it won't last five minutes with Sergio.' Kathy delivered that forecast with a shrug of a narrow shoulder to show how low her expectations were and reached for her jeans, intending to get changed. 'I think he's just curious about how the other half lives.'

'Will you tell him?'

Kathy paled and tensed. She knew immediately that Bridget was referring to the prison sentence that the younger woman had served. 'I don't think Sergio will be around long enough for a heartfelt confession to become necessary. But if he asks too many awkward questions, I won't lie—'

'Give things a chance to develop first,' Bridget advised hurriedly.

'He's too sophisticated and well travelled to fool. If I tried to pretend I spent all that time abroad I'd soon trip myself up,' Kathy countered gently.

'He's not going to ask for map references, Kathy,' the little brunette scolded. 'Don't go spilling it all out when there's no need. You're entitled to a few secrets until you know him better.'

Bridget was very much a romantic and Kathy

wouldn't have had her any other way, but Kathy had not been able to bring herself to the point of confessing to her friend that she had already been intimate with Sergio. In fact, the more Kathy thought about that, the more disturbed and ashamed she became over her behaviour. She was annoyed that she had not had more sense. The fear that there might be consequences from their contraceptive accident was one she kept pushed to the back of her mind; she was planning to do a pregnancy test in a couple of days.

Surprisingly, Sergio had actually phoned her four times since he had left London. He had called her from Norway and talked with astonishing enthusiasm about white-outs and skiable peaks. Whether he was telling her about living rough in a wilderness of snow fields, frozen lakes and forest or revealing an abiding passion for what she had discovered was the world's most expensive coffee, Sergio could be very entertaining.

Kathy had, however, satisfied her curiosity about him on the internet and had been both intrigued and troubled by what she learned. Born to an almost royal existence of extreme privilege in a vast Italian palazzo, Sergio had evidently led a charmed life until he became mysteriously estranged from his father while he was still at university. Although virtually disinherited in favour of his younger half-brother, Sergio had still contrived to make his first million by the age of twenty-two and he had hogged the fast lane of energetic high-powered achievement ever since. Super-rich and super-successful, he maintained the same hectic pace in his private life. He had a rather chilling reputation with women. When he wasn't doing his utmost to kill himself in dangerous sporting activities, he was staving off boredom with a relentless parade of beautiful women, all of whom belonged to the celebrity and socialite sets.

As Kathy caught the bus home from work the following evening, she was striving not to dwell too much on those unpalatable truths because, by finding her employment, Sergio had single-handedly contrived to transform her life. Her new job was in a busy advertising agency, which buzzed with activity at all hours of the day and she absolutely loved it. A quick learner, she had already been complimented on her work. It was the opportunity she had so badly needed to prove her ability and gain experience. But without Sergio's intervention she knew that she would not have been given that chance. That did not mean she planned to sleep with him when she saw him that night, but it did mean that she would probably continue to hold back and not beat him if they ever played chess again.

Amused by that idea, Kathy donned the citrus-yellow dress. A car collected her on the dot of eight and took her across the city to a very exclusive residential block. Shown into the lift by the driver, she was tense and uncomfortable. Where was she being taken? Not unnaturally she had assumed they were going out. Maybe he didn't want to take her anywhere. Maybe he was afraid that her table manners or appearance would let him down.

Bright coppery head held high, Kathy walked across the marble hall and through the open door facing her into a stunning reception room so large that it seemed to stretch into infinity. Her heartbeat was moving up tempo, colour warming her cheeks.

'Kathy…' Sergio strolled forward to greet her.

And the definitive word to describe him, she thought dizzily, was *gorgeous*. His fashionable suit was the colour of dark chocolate and, worn with a fawn T-shirt, it struck a wonderfully classic and casual note. Just one glimpse of the hard, masculine planes of his lean bronzed face unleashed the butterflies in her stomach. It took tremendous self-control for her to rise above those promptings and say out loud what was on her mind.

'Is this your apartment?' Kathy asked stiffly.

Sergio ran veiled dark eyes as cold as ice over her and, even though he was disgusted by what he now knew about her character, he still could not deny her stunning physical appeal. The bright yellow dress set off her glorious hair and her green eyes shone like polished jade against her pale porcelain complexion. He knew at a glance that the outfit was designer faux-vintage and had no doubt at all in deciding where she had got the money to buy it: from the sale of his watch.

'Yes. Why?' he tossed back smooth as glass.

'Are we going out?' Kathy asked tautly.

Sergio gazed steadily back at her. 'I thought we'd be more comfortable staying here.'

'Either we go out somewhere, or I go home.' Kathy tilted her chin and sent him a look of disdain, angry hurt and strong pride powering her. 'I'm not an easy option you call up when you feel like sex. If that's all you're interested in, I'm leaving. No offence intended.'

His dark scrutiny kindled to gold as though she had tossed a burning torch on a bale of hay and provoked a blaze. 'You can't leave until you've answered certain questions to my satisfaction.'

Kathy froze. 'What are you talking about?'

'Let's keep it simple. You stole my watch. I want to know what you did with it.'

'I…*stole* your watch? Are you crazy?' Kathy exclaimed, barely able to credit that accusation coming at her out of the blue. 'I remember you asking about it before you left London but—'

'You were the last person to see it in my office. It can scarcely be a coincidence that you should also have a criminal record for theft.'

Her delicate natural colour ebbed to leave her an ashen shade. Without warning he was plunging her back into the nightmare that she had believed she had left behind. He *knew* about her past. She felt sick and cornered, and under attack. He believed she was a thief and that only she could be responsible for the disappearance of his watch. For a few taut seconds her mind was in turmoil and her throat was so tight she could barely get oxygen into her lungs.

For an instant Sergio wondered if she might faint. She'd turned as white as snow, her pallor in stark contrast to her vivid hair and dress. She was terrified, of course she was. He did not regret choosing the short, sharp shock approach. He liked results and he liked them fast.

'I didn't steal your watch,' Kathy framed shakily.

'Are lies a wise move at this point?' Sergio traded, unimpressed. 'I could call the police right now and let them handle it. But I would prefer to deal with this in a private capacity. Keep two facts in mind: I have no pity for those who try to take advantage of me and I have never regarded women as the weaker sex.'

'I didn't touch your watch!' Her protest was vehement. A pulse was beating so fast at the base of her throat that still she found it difficult to catch her breath. That reference to the police terrified her, bringing back memories she would have done anything to forget and which she had no wish to relive. With her history as a former offender, how could she possibly hope to combat an accusation from a very rich and powerful man?

Sergio regarded her with cold, steady determination. 'I won't let you leave this apartment until you have told me the truth.'

'You can't do that!' Kathy told him in disbelief. 'You don't have the right.'

'Oh, I think you'll give me the right to do whatever I like, *cara mia*,' Sergio countered silkily. 'I believe that you will do virtually anything to keep the police out of this. Am I correct?'

As she received that very shrewd assumption Kathy's teeth almost chattered together. Yet, while fear was making her skin clammy, rage was sitting like a lump of red hot coal inside her. 'How did you find out that I had served a prison sentence?'

'My security chief started checking you out when he saw you making chess moves on the surveillance camera. He's very thorough.'

'Is he?' Kathy raised a fine brow in disagreement. 'I would say that I make a very convenient fall guy—'

'Renzo Catallone doesn't operate like that,' Sergio asserted. 'He used to be in the police force.'

'Even better!' A bitter laugh was wrenched from Kathy's dry throat before she could bite it back. 'He saw that I had a criminal record and that was that, wasn't it? Investigation over!'

'Are you denying that you stole the watch?'

'Yes, but clearly you don't believe me and I don't have any way of proving that I didn't take it. Obviously, you have a thief in your office. It might just be someone in a smart business suit, someone who was tempted, even someone who wanted a thrill. Thieves come in all shapes and sizes and in all walks of life.'

Sergio rested brooding dark eyes of derision on her. The crime for which she had once been convicted filled him with distaste. Far from being the refreshingly natural and unspoilt girl he had come to believe her to be, her beauty hid a rotten core of serious greed. In the position of carer and companion, she had abused the trust of an elderly invalid and had systematically robbed her charge over a period of many months. She had been prosecuted for the theft of the single item found in her possession, but she had almost certainly been responsible for stealing and disposing of other valuable antiques that had disappeared without trace during her employment.

'I don't need you to tell me the obvious,' Sergio responded drily. 'In this case I'm confident that I'm looking at the culprit.'

'But then you're confident in every sphere.' Kathy slowly shook her head. Her copper and amber hair glittered with bright streaks, forming a metallic halo that accentuated the pallor of her ivory complexion.

Dully she recognised that she was in shock. In the space of minutes he had torn her newly learnt self-belief to shreds. He had tempted her out of the safety of her quiet life only to threaten to destroy her. She hated him for it. She hated him for the arrogant assurance that convinced him that he was right and she was in the wrong. She hated herself for believing, however briefly, that she could aspire to dating a guy like him. What sort of an idiot had she become? Did she believe in fairy stories, as well? She had surrendered her defence mechanisms when she'd put on the pretty yellow dress. Within the anger and the fear lurked a very strong sense of humiliation.

'Let's keep this clean and straightforward. I want to know what you did with the watch,' Sergio repeated grimly. 'And don't waste my time with tears or tantrums. They don't work with me.'

An insidious chill ran down her taut spinal cord as she recorded the cruel lack of emotion stamped on his lean, dark, handsome features. He would never listen to her story of the injustice she had suffered—he would have neither the faith nor the patience. He had no time for her or her explanations, since he dealt in black and white facts. As far as he was concerned, she was a convicted thief and she might have served her sentence, but he was not prepared to give her the benefit of the doubt.

'I didn't take it, so I don't know where you expect to go with this. I haven't got the information you're asking for,' Kathy framed tightly.

Implacable dark as ebony eyes rested on her. 'Then I hand you over to the police.'

All Kathy could think about was the threat of being sent back to prison. For a split second she was back there in a cell with endless empty hours to fill without occupation or privacy. She was back in the grip of the powerlessness, the despair and the fear. The scar on her back seemed to pulse with remembered pain. Perspiration broke out on her short upper lip, gooseflesh on her exposed skin. Unlike Bridget's daughter, who had never come home again, Kathy had coped and she had survived. But the prospect of being forced to cope a second time with the loss of all freedom and dignity was too much for her to bear.

'I don't want that,' she admitted half under her breath.

'Neither do I,' Sergio confided lazily. 'Having to admit that I shagged the office cleaner would be tacky.'

Her facial muscles tightened at the insult, while her brain discarded the degrading words as an irrelevance. Her mind was on a frantic feverish search for any solution that might persuade him not to involve the police. Only something unusual was likely to appeal to Sergio Torrente. He liked danger and he liked risk and he loved to compete.

'If I can beat you at chess tonight, you let me walk away,' Kathy shot that proposition at him before she could lose her nerve.

That sudden turnaround in attitude took Sergio by surprise. In that one reckless sentence she'd acknowledged her guilt as a thief and bargained with him for her freedom. But she'd done both without apology or explanation. He found her audacity a turn-on. 'You're challenging me?'

Her green eyes were alight with defiance, but deep down inside she was a mass of panic and insecurity because she knew that she was literally fighting for the chance to keep her life from falling apart again. 'Why not?''

'What's in it for me? A good game?' Sergio derided. 'That watch was worth at least forty grand. You set a high rating on your entertainment value.'

Consternation gripped Kathy at that news. *Forty thousand* pounds? It had not occurred to her that the missing item might be so valuable. Her apprehension increased. 'The choice is yours.'

'If you lose, I want my watch back,' Sergio delivered with sardonic bite. 'Or, at the very least, the details of where it was disposed of.'

As he asked for the impossible again Kathy was careful not to meet his astute eyes in a direct collision. But his tacit agreement to her challenge sent the adrenalin zinging through her veins again, loosening the fierce tension in her spine and lower limbs. He would play her and whatever it took she had to win. If she lost she would be right back where she had started out, with the added disadvantage that he would be outraged when she was unable to provide either the watch or the information that might lead to its return.

'Okay,' Kathy agreed, toughing out the pretence that she could deliver that deal because he had given her no other choice.

'And I think that, whatever the result, I should enjoy a reprise of the best entertainment you can offer, *delizia mia*,' Sergio murmured, lifting the phone to request that a chess set be brought in.

Her fine brows pleated. 'Sorry?'

Sergio dealt her an appreciative glance. Her outfit gave her the tantalising femininity of a delicate tea rose but her suggestion that they play for what was, after all, *his* watch was as ingenious as it was in-your-face impudent. 'We finish the contest in bed.'

Kathy went rigid, colour splashing her wide, high cheekbones, anger rising and soaring high within her. She was shattered by that demand, for she thought it was utterly unfair. 'Regardless of who wins?'

'There has to be something extra in it for me.'

Kathy focused on the superb view through the nearest window and thought of the lack of view she would have in a cell. Her tummy flipped, her skin chilled at that realistic acknowledgement of who held the true power. He had the whip hand while she had only her wits as ammunition. 'All right.'

A manservant appeared with a polished antique wooden

box and laid out a board table with stylish carved chess pieces. A maid arrived to serve refreshments. Kathy took her seat. Even though she had not eaten since lunch time, she refused the offer of a drink and the tiny tempting canapés that accompanied it. It was all so civilised that she almost laughed out loud. On the face of it she was an honoured guest, but she knew she would be playing for her very survival.

Sergio lifted a white and then a black pawn and closed his hands round them. Kathy picked a fist and won white to play. She told herself it was a good omen and her concentration went into super mode. She had no sense of time, only of the patterns and combinations on the board in front of her. He was an aggressive player, who made a steady advance. But her strategy was more intricate, her moves lightning-fast to push up the pace. She let him capture her bishop and then slid her knight behind his.

'Check,' she breathed softly and a short while later she trapped his king.

'Checkmate,' Sergio conceded, stunned by the level of her brilliance and incensed that she had concealed the extent of her skill during their two previous games.

Kathy snatched in a slow quivering breath. It was over; she was safe. Her skin was damp with stress. Adrenalin was still pumping through her on a high octane charge. Pushing back her chair, she got up.

Dark golden eyes shimmering, Sergio followed suit. 'You fixed the tie last time we played,' he condemned.

'Maybe it was my way of flirting with you.' Kathy threw her head high, reacting to the electric tension in the air. 'Guys don't like being beaten, do they?'

'Some prefer a challenge,' Sergio traded.

'But you're not one of them,' Kathy dared with scorn. 'Your past features a remarkable number of airheads.'

'Horses for courses,' Sergio rhymed unabashed. 'Is this the real Kathy Galvin? Or is there yet another Kathy waiting in the wings? You're full of astonishing contradictions.'

Annoyed he had not reacted angrily to her taunt when she was keen to keep him at a distance, Kathy was non-committal. 'Am I?'

'A cleaner, when you could be a model. A virgin. A chess player, who could make an Olympic team, and a thief.' Sergio lifted a hand and laced lean brown fingers into the luxuriant thickness of her amber and copper streaked hair. 'I don't like what you are but you fascinate me, *cara mia.*'

His thumb stroked the delicate skin below her ear and she trembled. He was so close she could smell his cologne, a fragrance that had already acquired an aching familiarity that awakened her senses. The proximity of his lean, powerful body was impossible to ignore. Her mouth knew the taste of him. Her body was already remembering him and wantonly keen to relive the experience. Her breasts felt warm and heavy inside her bra. Her breath fluttered in her throat as she fought the treacherous demon of her own sensuality.

He tipped her head back. Merciless golden eyes assailed hers and forced a connection. 'You keep the watch…and tonight I keep you,' he reminded her with ruthless precision. 'But I don't want a martyr in my bed.'

Kathy had no intention of playing the victim and she was too proud to try and reason with him again. She knew how he operated. If she ruled the chessboard, he would rule the bedroom. She had made the deal and she refused to let herself think and react with her emotions: she was tougher than that. Life had gone wrong again, but she would handle it just as she had before, she told herself fiercely. He closed a hand over hers and led her into the hall and down a corridor.

The master bedroom suite overlooked a big roof garden. She could hardly credit that something as beautiful as that garden could exist so many floors above street level. She focused on it while he unzipped her dress and spread back its edges. Her heart starting to hammer like a road drill, she watched his reflection in the sunlit wall of glass. He bent his proud dark head and pressed his expert mouth to a narrow white shoulder blade. He found a place she didn't know existed and triggered a frisson of response that slivered through her, shocking her back into awareness of him.

Sergio laughed softly. 'I don't want a woman behaving like an exquisite automaton. I want you wide awake, *delizia mia*.'

'What do those words mean?' she whispered.

'My delight—and you are. Wildly inventive dreams about you have disturbed my sleep ever since I left London,' he confided thickly.

'So my being a thief really didn't make much difference to you?'

His big powerful frame tensed behind hers. He spun her round to look him. Forbidding dark eyes flared down into hers.

But Kathy was untouched by that silent censure. Indeed she was almost provoked by the anger she could feel contained within him, firmly controlled by self-discipline. 'You're more sensitive than you might seem.'

'Where is your shame?' he demanded.

'Are you ashamed that you are using your power over me to get me into bed again?'

Sergio dealt her a fulminating appraisal and then he

startled her with a shout of laughter. 'No,' he conceded, his strong, hard-boned face spectacularly handsome as grim amusement splintered his usual sombre mien. 'But then why would I be? You want me just as much.'

'Don't men always tell themselves ego-boosting stuff like th-that?' Her voice succumbed to a slight nervous jerk as he eased her dress down over her wrists and lifted her free of the rich brocade fabric as easily as if she were a doll.

In answer, Sergio bent his arrogant dark head and kissed her. The moist curl and flick of his tongue against the roof of her mouth made her shiver. The emotion she had walled up inside her burst out in a hungry surge. She wanted, wanted, *hated* wanting him, refused to surrender to it. As her defensive stiffness grew he gathered her close and tasted her soft pink lips with an intoxicating sweetness that was so unexpected it transfixed her. He followed that tantalising assault with a passionate urgency that sent sparks of fire dancing through her veins. With a roughened sound in his throat, he wrenched her bra out of his path and closed a hand over the silken soft curve of her breast. Her knees went weak, her body burning.

'You want me too,' Sergio husked against her reddened, love-bruised mouth. 'Admit it.'

'No!' Her green eyes flashing like polished emeralds, she pulled free. Picking up the yellow dress, she shook it out and laid it carefully across a chair.

'Even though it might pay to please me?' Sergio traded, smooth as silk.

'You get one night and that's it—you don't ever come near me again!' Kathy hissed back at him like a bristling cat. 'You got that?'

'I got it, *delizia mia*,' Sergio intoned, sweeping her up

into his arms to carry her over to the bed. 'Whether or not I'll accept it is another question. I dislike doing what other people tell me.'

'Tell me something I don't know.' Finding herself sprawled on the bed clad only in her briefs, Kathy became suddenly less strident. Uncomfortable with her semi-unclothed state, she flung a look of dismay at the sunlit windows. 'For goodness' sake, close the curtains!'

Amused by that sudden lurch from feisty cool to panic, Sergio hit a button and flicked another to put on the lights. He shed his jacket and his tie while he watched her with the single-minded golden gaze of a predator. Her beautiful eyes were wary, her colourful hair tousled. He recognised her extraordinary magnetism. On his bed she was as unusual and exotic as a tiger strolling through a drawing room.

Beneath that forceful scrutiny, Kathy was uneasy and she twisted away to conceal her bare breasts. Her shyness infuriated her, for she saw it as yet another weakness and her conscience was already shouting at her. She had kissed him back with more than toleration. How could she have responded with that much enthusiasm to a guy she loathed? On the other hand, wasn't it as well that she could? But *why* could she still respond to him?

'*Madonna mia,*' Sergio was staring in shock at the jagged scar that marred the white skin of her back. 'What the hell happened to you?'

When Kathy realised what had grabbed his attention she thrust herself back against the pillows so that that part of her body was hidden again. She was mortified that he should have seen the ugly evidence of the attack she had suffered three years earlier. 'Nothing—'

'That was not nothing—'

Her vivid green eyes were screened, her lithe, slender length taut. 'But I don't have to talk about it if I don't want to.'

Clad in designer boxers, Sergio came down on the bed. He was tall, bronzed and boldly masculine, his powerful muscles laid over the lean, strong frame of an athlete. 'Are you always this ready for a fight?'

Kathy was feeling incredibly tense. 'If you don't like it, send me home.'

Dark golden eyes intent, Sergio stared down at her with the aggressive potency of a hunter. She couldn't take her attention from him. In response, he curved lean fingers to the nape of her neck. 'Maybe I could get to like fighting, *delizia mia*,' he husked, tipping up her mouth to the wide, sensual promise of his.

Her nerves were as lively as jumping beans; she was rigid. But the kiss was a teasing provocation that enticed and promised. Her breath feathered in her throat. The taste of him intoxicated her but she fought that truth, determined to endure his attentions rather than respond to him. He found the delicate swell of her breasts and massaged the velvet peaks to sensitive rosebud crests. Arrows of exquisite sensation were slivering through her. But still she struggled to withstand his sexual mastery.

Sergio tugged her down into his arms to combat her resistance. There was more urgency than patience in the possessive stroke of his hands over her slender curves. There was greater demand in the heated force of his mouth. She twisted and turned beneath the onslaught of his increasing ardour. No matter how hard she tried to stay separate he was sweeping her up into the same storm of passion where pride had no place and only fervent need ruled.

'You want me too,' he told her thickly. 'It's reciprocal. I saw it in you the first time you looked at me.'

Her lashes swept down to conceal her apple-green eyes. She wouldn't answer but she was powerless to control the desire he had aroused. Her fingers were digging into his wide brown shoulders. The aromatic scent of his skin entranced her. At first meeting he had imprinted on her senses and she had recognised him on every level since then. The bewildering strength of that initial bonding scared her and infuriated her but it also exhilarated her.

'You are so stubborn,' Sergio growled in the simmering silence.

'I'm not here to stroke your ego!' Kathy declared.

He ground her lips apart with devouring heat and punished her with pleasure. Every nerve-ending in her body leapt in response. He worked his erotic path down over her squirming length, lingering on the rosy crowns of her breasts with his tongue and his teeth and exploring the hidden places to discover the exquisite sensitivity of her most tender flesh. The excitement became overwhelming. Her heart pounded in her eardrums, for in no time at all the yearning became a ravenous need. His caresses pushed her to an edge of frustrated torment that she found unbearable.

'Sergio…'

'Say please,' he urged breathlessly.

She gritted her teeth. 'No!'

'Some day I'll make you say please,' he swore.

But Kathy wasn't listening. Trembling with desire, she was already pulling him closer. Hot and impatient, Sergio required little encouragement. Golden eyes ablaze, he slid between her thighs and entered her with energising heat and strength. She cried out in startled acknowledgement of his invasion. He had made her burn with an irresistible hunger and now the dark, delirious pleasure began. It was glorious and her capacity for enjoyment knew no limits. His passionate intensity drove her wild with excitement. Sensation gradually became a raw, sweet agony until he sent her careening to a tumultuous peak of explosive release.

There was a timeless moment of pure ecstasy and joy. In the sensual ripples of delight that followed, she felt wonderfully close to him, transformed and at peace. And then her brain kicked back into action and blew all those fine feelings away again. She remembered how things really were between them and felt angry, mortified and earth-shatteringly bitter. As a deep sense of hurt threatened to surface she squashed it flat and wrenched herself free of his arms in a fierce gesture of rejection.

'Can I leave now?' Kathy asked, snaking over to the far side of the bed and sliding her legs off the edge with an eagerness to depart that spoke more clearly than any words. 'Or are you really going to insist I stay the whole night?'

Sergio was accustomed to women who voiced compliments and witty remarks in the aftermath of intimacy. He thought her attitude offensive.

Kathy didn't wait for an answer from him. She rose upright in a hurry and was quite unprepared for the wave of dizziness that engulfed her. The room tilted in front of her bemused eyes and the floor threatened to rise and greet her. Her face damp with perspiration, she swayed and staggered before she sank hurriedly back down on the bed again.

'What's wrong?' he asked.

Kathy was fighting an attack of nausea while taking slow, deep breaths in a desperate effort to clear her swimming head. 'Maybe I stood up too fast.'

'Lie down.' Sergio pressed her back against the pillows. 'I thought you were going to faint.'

'I haven't eaten in hours. That's all that's wrong,' she muttered, feeling foolish at having her big exit halted in its tracks. 'I'll be fine in a minute.'

'I'll order food.' Sergio used the phone by the bed and began getting dressed.

Kathy refused to look at him. 'I just want to go home.'

'As soon as you've eaten something and you're feeling better.' Lean, dark face sombre, Sergio spoke with scrupulous politeness.

Gripped by an overwhelming weariness that was as unfamiliar to her as the dizziness, Kathy swallowed hard and said nothing. She knew that there was no way she was going to feel better in the near future. He had destroyed her peace of mind and devastated her pride. What if her worst fear came true and she was pregnant? Pregnant by a guy whom she hated like poison?

CHAPTER FIVE

THE next morning, Kathy woke up feeling sick again.

Although she was afraid of using the pregnancy test she had bought too soon and wasting it, her nerves would no longer stand the prospect of a longer wait. It shook her that it took so little time to perform a test that was of earth-shattering importance to her life. A few minutes later and she had the result that she had dreaded: she was going to have a baby. Her tummy flipped with panic and nausea and she had to make a dash for the bathroom. In the aftermath, even a morsel of toast was more than her tender digestive system could contemplate.

Had she but known it, Sergio was not having a very satisfactory start to his day, either. He had only just arrived at the Torrente building when his senior executive PA, Paola, and his security chief, Renzo Catallone, requested an urgent meeting with him.

Paola laid the watch that Sergio had never expected to see again down on his desk. 'I'm really sorry, sir. I'm very upset about this. I came into the office very early on the morning I went on holiday because I wanted to check that I'd taken care of everything before I left. I saw your watch lying on the floor of your office and I locked it in a drawer in my desk for safe keeping—'

'*You* found my watch?' Sergio interrupted with incredulity. 'And said nothing?'

'I was in a hurry to leave. There was nobody else around. I did email another staff member to say where your watch was, but evidently the message was overlooked,' the troubled brunette explained unhappily. 'When I came back to work this morning, someone mentioned that your watch had gone missing and that everyone thought it had been stolen. It was only then that I realised that nobody knew what I'd done.'

That morning, Kathy could not help noticing every pregnant woman in her vicinity and she was amazed by how many of them there seemed to be. Even though the reality of her predicament had yet to sink in she could feel panic waiting to pounce on her. Other women managed to cope with unplanned pregnancies and so would she, she told herself doggedly. She had to consider all the options open to her and stay calm. But if she chose to be a single parent she would not be able to manage without financial help—*his* financial help. That lowering prospect made Kathy stiffen with distaste. She could not forget Sergio Torrente's crack about how having his child would be a 'lucrative lifestyle choice.'

'Call for you,' Kathy was told by her colleague on Reception.

'Why are you not answering your mobile?' Sergio enquired, his rich dark drawl thrumming down the line and paralysing her to the spot.

'I'm not allowed to take personal calls. I'm sorry I can't talk to you,' Kathy told him flatly and cut the connection, furious that he had dared to phone her. Was there no limit to his arrogance? Was he incapable of appreciating that she wanted nothing to do with him? The night before he had left her in peace to get dressed and eat the meal that was brought to her. She had travelled home in a limo and cried herself to sleep. Of course, she would have to speak to him sooner or later, she acknowledged reluctantly. But just then later had much more appeal to her than sooner.

Mid-morning a spectacular designer flower arrangement was delivered to her. Kathy opened a card signed only with Sergio's initials. Why was he phoning her and sending her flowers? Uncomfortably aware of the amount of attention the extravagant vase of exotic tiger lilies and grasses was generating, she tried to hand it back to the delivery man. 'I'm sorry but I don't want this—'

'That's not my problem,' he told her and off he went.

An hour later, another phone call came from Sergio, but she refused to take it. At noon, her supervisor approached her and took her aside to speak to her in a low voice. 'You can take extra time for your lunch break today. In fact, I've been told to tell you that it'll be fine if you want to take the rest of the afternoon off.'

Kathy studied her in bewilderment. 'But why?'

'The boss received a special request from the CEO. I believe Mr Torrente's driver is waiting outside for you.'

Kathy flushed to the roots of her hairline. She wanted to sink through the floor. But as she parted her lips to protest that she did not wish to see Sergio and had no wish whatsoever to be singled out for special treatment the other woman went into retreat, her uneasiness palpable. Sergio had the subtlety of a ram-raider, Kathy thought in outraged embarrassment as she squirmed beneath the covert glances and low-pitched buzz of comment that accompanied her departure from the agency. What Sergio wanted he had to have and he refused to wait.

Fizzing with fierce resentment, Kathy climbed into the waiting Mercedes. Should she tell him that she was pregnant? Or did she need to deal with her own feelings before she made an announcement? Fifteen minutes later, she was set down in front of an exclusive hotel. A doorman ushered her into the opulent interior. One of Sergio's bodyguards greeted her in the foyer and escorted her into the lift. She was shown into a palatial reception room.

Sergio strolled through the balcony doors that stood ajar and came to a fluid halt. As an entrance it was unrivalled in the performance stakes, for he was a dazzlingly good-looking guy. Her heart jumped and her breath shortened in her throat. No matter how she felt about Sergio, or how often she saw him, his physical impact did not lessen. Her response was involuntary. She looked at him and she knew she would look again and again and again. It was as if some wanton, rebellious sixth sense of hers had already forged a permanent connection with him.

'What do I say?' His dark drawl as rich and smooth as vintage wine, Sergio spread graceful lean brown hands. 'I am rarely at a loss, but I don't know what to say to you—'

'Well, believe me, I'm not stuck for words!' Kathy broke in to tell him roundly. 'How dare you put me in a position where I had no choice but to come here and see you? I liked my job. But what you did today—going to the boss to demand that I get out of work—was the equivalent of career suicide!'

'I needed to see you and I made a polite request. Don't exaggerate.'

'I'm not exaggerating.' Her apple-green eyes were

bright with indignation. 'I didn't know that you owned the advertising agency, as well as the recruitment company. A request from the CEO is the same as a demand. Now you've made it obvious that we have some kind of personal connection, I'll be the equivalent of a plague-carrier at work! After this, nobody's going to take me seriously and my colleagues will be counting the days until my temporary contract ends.'

Sergio expelled his breath on a measured hiss. 'If there is a problem, I'll secure employment for you elsewhere.'

Her slim white hands knotted into fists of frustration. 'Nothing is that simple. Is that really all you have to say?'

'No. I had to see you today to apologise.' His astute dark eyes were level and unflinching. 'My watch was not stolen, it was misplaced. Please accept my sincere regrets for accusing you of something which you did not do.'

That change of subject and the information that his watch had been found momentarily distracted Kathy and her brows pleated.

'But there is one thing that I cannot understand,' Sergio continued with a slow shake of his handsome dark head. 'Why on earth did you admit to stealing my watch in the first place?'

'What else could I do? You didn't believe me when I told you I hadn't taken it!'

'You didn't persist in pleading your innocence for very long. When you offered to play me for my watch, I naturally took it as a confession of guilt and I acted accordingly.'

'You acted *appallingly*.' Anger drove colour up over Kathy's slanted cheekbones as she voiced that contradiction.

'I'm not a soft touch. If you offend me I fight back. Circumstances weren't in your favour. You are a convicted thief and it did colour my judgement.' Sergio traded that defence without hesitation. 'But if you had not challenged me to that game on the terms that you did, I would not have slept with you last night.'

Kathy trembled with rage. 'So, even though you have apologised, it's really all my own fault?'

'That was not what I said. I fired my security chief over this affair today—'

'The ex-policeman? You gave him the sack for jumping to the same conclusion about me that you did?' Kathy exclaimed in disgust. 'How can you be so unjust?'

Disconcerted by that reaction, Sergio breathed, 'Unjust? How?'

'Unlike you, that man never met me and had no personal knowledge of me. He was only doing his job. You should blame yourself for misjudging me, not him.'

'Your compassion for Renzo surprises me. Why don't we discuss our differences over lunch?'

'I'd have to be starving to eat with you!' Kathy flung back, unimpressed.

'I love your passion, but I am less fond of drama, *cara mia*.'

Powerful dissatisfaction gripped Kathy, for she felt like a wave trying to batter a granite rock into subjection. He was stonewalling her. Her accusations had washed clean off him again. Her pain and anger were rising in direct proportion to her inability to break through his ice cool façade. 'Last night I was afraid you would call the police. I was terrified of ending up back in jail. That's the only reason I slept with you and I truly *hate* you for it—'

'You're angry with me. I accept that and I'm prepared to make amends by whatever means are within my power. But I do not accept that you only shared my bed out of fear.'

Fury roared through Kathy in an energising flood. 'Of course, you're going to say that!'

'But we both know that that claim is untrue.' Sergio rested glittering golden eyes on her in a challenging look as scorching as his touch.

The atmosphere was electric.

Kathy was so tense her muscles ached. Her heart thumped inside her tight chest. She sucked in a ragged breath. 'Don't tell me what I know.'

'Then admit the obvious. The sexual chemistry between us is extraordinarily strong. Don't you know how rare it is to feel this much excitement just being in the same room with someone?' Sergio murmured huskily.

Her legs felt weak and wobbly. The butterflies were back in her tummy and her mouth was running dry. 'That doesn't matter—'

'It always matters.'

A fleeting encounter with his brilliant predatory gaze pierced her with a flood of erotic awareness. The sensitive peaks of her breasts tingled. She remembered the taste and the urgency of his mouth on hers. Her slender hands tightened into defensive fists. Excitement was like a dangerous drug in her veins, powering a sensual awakening. She shivered in the grip of that madness and fought her weakness with all her might, her anger surfacing again. 'I don't want anything more to do with you—'

'But if I touched you now you'd burn up in my arms, *delizia mia*,' Sergio savoured that forecast with blazing assurance.

'Don't even think of getting that close!' Her reaction was raw in tone. 'I'm not stupid. I know how you think of me. You were too quick to remind me today that I'm a convicted thief. You said that in virtually the same breath as you apologised for accusing me of stealing your watch.'

Sergio rested unrepentant dark eyes on her. 'I won't lie or prevaricate. How do you expect me to feel about your history as a former offender? It's not acceptable. How could it be?'

Kathy was stunned to feel a prickly surge of tears threatening the backs of her eyes. She wasn't the tearful sort, but around him she was not her rational self and her emotions were in a chaotic tangle. How would he react when she told him that regardless of her shameful history she had conceived his child? Just then she couldn't handle the thought or the prospect of that humiliation. She focused studiously on the balcony where she could see the corner of a table and a crystal wineglass. 'I hope I'm getting a lift back to work,' she said tightly. 'I only get an hour for lunch and I'm already late.'

'I want you to stay,' Sergio spelt out.

'You can't always have what you want.' Kathy was struggling to control the see sawing thoughts and feelings attacking her in waves. 'Things have become more complicated than you appreciate.'

'What things?' Impatience stamped his lean dark features and his intonation.

His only use for her was sexual, Kathy thought in bitter mortification. But no doubt his ease of conquest had encouraged that attitude and she knew she could not blame him entirely for that. Even so, the base line was that he had the blue-blooded arrogance of wealth and privilege and her criminal conviction made her the lowest of the low in his eyes. That would never, ever change. She wondered why she was holding back on telling him that she was pregnant, for the passage of time would alter nothing. Indeed, she reasoned heavily, breaking the bad news and giving him the chance to come to terms with the idea was probably the more dignified plan of action to follow.

'I'm pregnant,' Kathy told him flatly. 'I did the test at home this morning.'

The silence that fell was bottomless, absolute and endless to her fast fraying nerves.

The instant she spoke, Sergio had veiled his keen dark gaze. His olive skin took on a faint ashen tone that she put down to shock. But that was his sole visible reaction, for his reserve and self-discipline triumphed. 'A doctor should check out that result,' he drawled without inflection. 'I'll organise it right now.'

Disconcerted by his cold-blooded calm, Kathy gave an uncertain nod of agreement. He was already using the phone and a few minutes later he told her that he had arranged a private medical appointment.

'If it's confirmed, have you any idea what you want to do?' Sergio enquired.

Her tension increased at that warning glimpse of a guy who preferred to solve every problem at speed. 'I don't want a termination,' she said in a taut undertone, feeling that it was only fair to tell him that up front.

'I wasn't going to suggest that option.' Sergio escorted her from the suite.

Lunch, she noted, was no longer on his agenda. In the lift, she said awkwardly, 'You don't need to come with me to see the doctor.'

'We're in this together.'

'The doctor can confirm the result. That's all you need to know at this stage.'

'I was trying to be supportive.'

Kathy shrugged a narrow shoulder, reluctant to be drawn. She didn't trust him. She didn't want to be put under pressure. The very fact that he was being careful not to betray his true feelings about her condition put her on her guard.

'I'll see you tonight, then,' Sergio conceded.

'I'd like a few days to think over all this.'

'How many days?'

As the uneasy silence thundered Sergio closed a hand over hers. 'Kathy…' he prompted.

'I'll phone you.' She tugged her fingers free from his, setting a boundary as much for her own benefit as for his. Although he did not voice his dissatisfaction the atmosphere had acquired a distinct chill.

Little more than an hour later, the smoothly spoken middle-aged gynaecologist confirmed that she was pregnant and warned her that she was underweight. A nurse gave her a sheaf of advisory leaflets. There and then, the new life Kathy carried within her began to seem rather more real to her. Back at the advertising agency she tried not to seem conscious of the curious looks she was receiving and the sudden silences when she passed by. Quite deliberately, she stayed late to make up the time she had missed over lunch.

The following morning when she arrived at work a colourful weekly gossip magazine was lying on her chair. Carefully folded open at the relevant page, it showed Sergio emerging from a New York nightclub with a famous young film actress clinging to him for support. A voluptuous blonde, Christabel Janson was reportedly very taken with her latest lover. Her throat so tight that it ached and her mood plummeting, Kathy forced a smile onto her lips that felt like concrete and dropped the magazine into the bin. Well, that was that. Someone had done her a favour in drawing that picture to her attention. It had certainly nipped any foolish expectations or romantic fancies in the bud. She might be expecting Sergio Torrente's child, but that really was the sum total of any continuing relationship that they now had.

That evening when Kathy took her break at the café, she told Bridget everything.

During that confessional, Bridget made several brusque comments about Sergio and gave the younger woman a reassuring hug. 'Falling pregnant is not the end of the world, so stop talking as though it is—'

Kathy gulped. 'I'm terrified—'

'It's the shock. Not to mention the fright Sergio Torrente gave you when he assumed that you had stolen his watch,' Bridget muttered tight-mouthed. 'When I think of what you've already gone through, his attitude makes my blood boil.'

'At least he was honest,' Kathy muttered heavily. 'But I hate him for it. How fair is that?'

'Forget about him. I'm more concerned about you.'

'Why am I crying all the time?' Kathy lamented, hauling out a tissue to mop at her overflowing eyes.

'Hormones,' Bridget answered succinctly.

Over the next forty-eight hours Kathy discovered two missed calls from Sergio on her mobile and she kept it switched off because she didn't want to speak to him. That evening she had an unexpected visitor when Renzo Catallone knocked on the door of her bedsit.

'I'd like to speak to you. Will you give me five minutes?' the former police officer asked bluntly.

Pale and stiff with unease, Kathy gave him a grudging nod.

'Mr Torrente has given me my job back as his chief of security,' Renzo volunteered. 'I understand that I have you to thank for that change of heart.'

Kathy was astonished by that assurance. 'But I only pointed out that it wasn't fair to blame you for misjudging me when you didn't actually know me.'

'In the circumstances, it was very generous of you to make that point on my behalf,' the older man told her warmly. 'I wanted to thank you and tell you that if there is ever anything I can do for you, please don't hesitate to ask for my help.'

Kathy went to bed that night feeling a little more cheerful and a little less ashamed of the past she could not change. The next day was Saturday, and she was serving breakfast at the café when Sergio strode in. His hard dark gaze raked across the room and closed in on her with punitive force. For a split second she stared and the edge-of-the-seat excitement was there, instant and powerful, sizzling through her slender taut frame like an electric charge. Her face flamed and she hastened into the kitchen with her order and lingered there.

Bridget put her head round the door. 'Kathy? We'll have to do without you today. Let Sergio take you home.'

'Bridget, I—'

'You have to talk to him some time.'

Kathy supposed that that was true. But it did mean stifling a seething desire to storm out and tell Sergio exactly what she thought of his two-timing cheating habits. With a baby on the way, she needed to take a long-term view, she told herself doggedly. Sergio was single and he could do as he liked. Her pregnancy was an accidental development. Now that the intimate side of things was over between them, establishing a civil connection with the future father of her child made better sense. Having given herself that quick mental pep talk, she emerged from the rear of the café clutching her bag and jacket.

The epitome of cool elegance in a black business suit teamed with a gold silk tie, Sergio was poised by the cash desk and incongruously out of step with his pedestrian surroundings. A bodyguard stood by the door, while two more hovered on the pavement outside.

Dark deep-set eyes alert, Sergio studied Kathy. As thin and pale as a wraith with her vibrant copper and red hair anchored in a casual pony-tail and her apple-green eyes hostile, she looked barely out of her teens. Yet not one of those facts detracted in the slightest from the power of her haunting beauty.

'You were supposed to wait for me to phone,' Kathy complained as she got into the limousine.

'That's not my style,' Sergio murmured lazily, the smoky timbre of his dark drawl ensuring that she remained outrageously aware of his sensual charisma. 'You need to collect your passport—we're flying to Paris this morning.'

Already shaken, her studied air of detachment evaporated entirely at that statement. 'Paris? Is this a joke?'

'No.'

'But to go all that way just for one day and when I'm supposed to be working…' Her voice ran out of steam because the minute she thought about it, the more she wanted to do it.

Sergio elevated a fine ebony brow. 'Why not? We have to talk and you're stressed. I would like you to relax today.'

CHAPTER SIX

THE opulent interior of Sergio's very large private jet took Kathy's breath away.

The main cabin was furnished with inviting seating areas and adorned with modern art. The interior also offered a purpose-built office, a movie theatre and several *en suite* bedrooms. In her casual beige corduroy jacket and denim jeans, she felt seriously at odds with the cutting-edge style of her surroundings.

'Wherever I am I have to be able to work. I spend a lot of time travelling and I usually have several staff with me,' Sergio explained over the delicious lunch that was prepared for them by his personal chef.

By the time the meal was over the jet was getting ready to land, for it was a very short flight.

'Why Paris?' Kathy asked in the limo that ferried them away from the hustle and bustle of CDG airport.

'France has strict press privacy laws. Many public figures find the media less intrusive here and a private life is more easily maintained,' Sergio advanced smoothly.

'So where are you taking me?'

'It's a surprise—a pleasant one, I hope, *cara mia*.'

Their destination was the island of Ile St-Louis, one of the most exclusive residential areas in Paris. The car came to a halt on a picturesque tree-lined quay in front of an elegant seventeenth-century building. Her curiosity rising by the second, Kathy accompanied Sergio inside. Sunlight fell from the tall windows and illuminated an elegant hall and staircase complemented by strikingly contemporary décor.

'Feel free to explore,' Sergio murmured softly.

Kathy made no attempt to hide her bewilderment. 'What's going on? Why have you brought me to this house?'

'I have bought this house for you. I want you to raise my child here.'

Kathy was stunned by the concept and the wording. *My* child, not our child. She noted the distinction but tried to regard it as an encouraging sign of his wish to be involved in his baby's future. Slowly she shook her head, her glorious hair sparkling like polished metal in the intense light, her green eyes alive with incredulity. 'You want me to move to another country and live as your dependant? Am I supposed to clap my hands with joy, or something?'

'Let me explain how I see this,' Sergio urged.

Kathy swallowed back another outburst on the score of his single-minded arrogance and audacity. She understood that she was supposed to be impressed to death by the sheer grandeur and expense of a surprise that must have cost him millions. Maybe he thought he was being clever, generous and creative in a difficult situation. Maybe he believed that she was a problem that could best be cured with a liberal shower of money. Regardless, she felt humiliated and offended as once again he contrived to underscore the differences of wealth, class and status between them while insisting on making all her choices for her.

'Some wine?' Sergio suggested, indicating the bottle

with the elegant label on the table. 'It's a classic Brunello from the Azzarini vineyards, which have belonged to the Torrentes for centuries.'

Her generous mouth compressed. 'I'm pregnant… alcohol is not supposed to be a good idea,' she extended when he continued to view her without comprehension. 'Don't you know anything about pregnant women?'

Sergio frowned. 'Why would I?'

Kathy folded her arms. 'Tell me why you think it would be a good idea for me to move to France.'

'If you remain in London, you will always be handi-capped by your past.'

'My prison record, you mean.' Her tummy gave a nauseous lurch as if reacting to her sudden increased tension and discomfiture.

Lean, strong face grim, Sergio surveyed her with level dark golden eyes. 'With my help you can rewrite that his-tory and bury your past. You can change your name and move here to embark on a new life. It would be a second chance for you and it would also provide a less contentious background for my child.'

His candour really hurt. Sucking in a steadying gulp of air, Kathy walked over to the window. Her nails were biting purple crescents into her palms as she fought to retain her composure. 'And you think that that's what I should do?'

'If you remain in London our association will inevitably be exposed by the press. Once that particular genie gets out of its bottle, it can't be put back.'

In an abrupt movement, Kathy spun back. 'I've listened to you, and now you have to listen to me. I went to prison for a crime I didn't commit. I did not steal that jug, or any of the other stuff that vanished from Mrs Taplow's collection.'

Dark as midnight eyes cool and uncompromising, Sergio released his breath on a long slow hiss. 'You made a mistake. You were very young and you had no family support system. Let's move on from there and deal with the current challenge.'

Losing colour, Kathy stared back at him. She was cut to the quick by his flat refusal to even consider that she might be innocent. 'Can't you even give me a fair hearing?'

'You had that hearing in a court of law before a judge and jury four years ago.'

Pale as death at that hard-hitting response, Kathy looked away from him, feeling as though he had slapped her in the face. She tried to open a door but he slammed it shut and then locked it for good measure. He refused to listen to her claim of innocence. He wasn't interested in hearing her story because he was convinced of her guilt.

'My concern relates to the future,' Sergio continued. 'Let's stay on track.'

Her vivid green eyes clashed head on with his, her anger unhidden. 'You're not concerned about me, except in so far as you want to control my every move without making a commitment in return.'

'This house is quite a commitment for me. Think of the life you could have here.' Sergio closed the distance between them to reach for her knotted hands and enclose them in his. 'A fresh start, no financial worries, the best of everything for you and your child. Why are you arguing about this? These practicalities have to be dealt with before we can consider any more personal angle.'

'I told you that I would *never* go for the "lucrative life-style choice" option.' Her voice was jerky because she was trying without success to work up the will-power to step back from him. On every level her senses craved physical contact, even if it was only the masculine warmth of his hands on hers. She was in total turmoil, wanting to do the right thing while being terrified of making the wrong decision.

'I should never have made that comment, *delizia mia*. I was on edge that evening and aggressive without cause. You are now carrying my child. Who else should take care of you?'

Sergio was so close she could see the ring of bronze that accentuated his dark pupils, the spiky ebony lashes that lent his gaze such mesmerising depth and impact. Antagonism and hurt slivered through her like warring wounding blades. She could hardly breathe for wanting him. There was a quivering knot of intense longing locked inside her. She could feel the euphoric effect of his proximity threatening to shut down her brain cells, as she had no desire to think or to deny herself or to drive a further wedge between them. It was an abysmal moment to appreciate that her feelings for Sergio Torrente ran much deeper than she had been prepared to admit.

'Kathy,' Sergio husked in an intonation that was pure predatory enticement.

'Look, I haven't even decided if I'm going to keep this baby yet.' Kathy had to force out that statement, because it took that much effort to think straight and suppress an acknowledgement that threatened to tear her apart with self-loathing.

As Sergio froze in surprise his lean brown fingers tightened round her narrow wrists. 'What are you trying to suggest?'

Her oval face defensive and deeply troubled, she pulled free of his hold. 'I may yet choose adoption—'

'Adoption?' Sergio was shattered by the word and the concept.

'I was adopted and I had a very happy childhood. If I'm not certain that I can give as much to my baby, I will consider adoption as a possibility. Because one thing I *do* know!' Kathy reasoned in a surge of heartfelt emotion. 'This is not about houses and appearances and money! Nor is it about what you want. It's about my ability to love and care for my baby!'

His lean, darkly handsome face clenched taut. 'Of course it is. But you will not be alone in that undertaking. You will have my support.'

'You won't be here for the tough stuff. You'll stay in the background and you'll visit only when it suits you to do so. Can't you understand that I don't want to be a hanger-on in your world? I don't want you paying my bills and telling me what to do at every turn—'

'That is not how it would be.'

Kathy was quick to challenge him again. 'No? So I'd be free to move another guy in here if I met one?'

His dark eyes flamed sizzling gold. He was taken by surprise and his hostile distaste to that idea spoke for him.

'Obviously not. You would expect me to live like a nun—'

'Or content yourself with me.'

'Oh…' Kathy trembled, tension forming like an iron bar in her spine as her rage climbed. 'So you're not just talking about being an occasional supportive parent. There would be sexual strings attached to this arrangement, as well.'

'That's a tacky observation. I can't see into the future. I don't know where we're going.' Sergio lifted a shoulder in a sophisticated shrug. Intensely charismatic, he was Italian to his manicured fingertips, but he was also cool as ice under pressure and he refused to be drawn into dangerous waters.

'You know exactly where we'd be going and that would be nowhere,' Kathy condemned shakily. 'From what I can work out, you haven't been in a relationship that went anywhere in living memory. And you're certainly not going to break that habit for a convicted thief!'

Sergio cornered her between the window and the wall and studied her with smouldering golden sensuality. 'Even if I can't keep my hands off you when you're annoying the hell out of me, *delizia mia*?'

But Kathy was too afraid of his magnetism to relax her guard for a moment. 'Did you tell Christabel Janson that too? Or did she qualify for a less critical approach?'

The classic lines of his hard-boned features were impassive while the teasing light had evaporated from his astute gaze. 'Don't go there,' he advised. 'I don't answer to any woman.'

'Then where do you get the nerve to demand anything from me?' Kathy was so incensed she was shaking. 'I absolutely refuse to be some dirty secret in your life!'

His stunning eyes flamed gold. 'I did not ask you to be.'

'Yes, you did. You're ashamed of me but you still want to sleep with me. I won't accept that *ever*. You wasted my time and yours bringing me here,' Kathy flung at him furiously and she stalked back to the door. 'I want to go back to London.'

'This is childish, *bellezza mia*.'

Kathy sent him a shimmering emerald glance, afraid to let go of her anger in case it weakened her. 'No, I'm being sensible.'

'We have to agree a way forward.'

Kathy dealt him a fiery appraisal. 'I can't talk to you

feeling like this—maybe we could talk on the phone and be polite in a few months' time.'

'In a few months?' Sergio splintered in raw disbelief at that liberal time frame. 'You need me *now*!'

'No, I don't.'

'*Maremma maiale*…you're not even looking after yourself properly!' Sergio condemned without warning. 'How many hours a day are you working? You can't keep up two jobs while you're pregnant and stay healthy.'

Kathy gave him a frozen look. 'I'll cope and I'll manage. I learned a long time ago not to rely on a man.'

'Who taught you that?'

'The love of my life—Gareth.' Her lush pink mouth curled as she deliberately stoked that bitterness to make it into a further barrier between them. 'We grew up next door to each other. There's nothing I wouldn't have done for him. But he was no use at all in a tight corner and you're not going to be any different—'

Outrage flashed in Sergio's hard-boned features. 'I'm doing everything possible to support you.'

'No, you're throwing money at me and trying to ship me out to a foreign country where I am less likely to cause you embarrassment. If that's what you call support, you can keep it!' Kathy reached out to open the front door in an effort to end the confrontation.

'*Madonna diavolo!* What about this? Will you do without this, as well?' Sergio caught her into his arms and crushed her soft full mouth beneath his with a passion that devastated her resistance.

He knotted one hand into her copper hair to hold her fast and clamped her slender body to his like a second skin. His heart pounded against hers. Urgently aware of his masculine arousal, she quivered in that hard embrace and exchanged kiss for kiss with a hunger as fierce, hot and lethal as a fever. But nothing could assuage the sadness within her and the ache at the heart of her. When he let her go she staggered back against the wall.

'I was supposed to drink the classic wine and go upstairs with you to celebrate, wasn't I?' Kathy was still fighting even though her knees didn't feel up to the challenge of holding her upright. 'But I'm not so desperate that I need to share a man and I never will be!'

Sergio was already using his phone. He did not deign to reply to that sally. His detachment was as effective as an invisible wall. The silence was suffocating. She felt shut out, pushed away and she found it unbearable. Even when she was so mad with him that she could have screamed she wanted to be back in his arms. He flipped the key to the door. She gave him a tiny split second to speak. He said nothing. He did nothing to prevent her from leaving, either.

'I hate you—I really, *really* hate you,' she whispered fierily as she left and, in that instant, she meant every word of it.

The door snapped shut behind her. There was not even the suspicion of a slam.

Conscious that Sergio's protection team were watching her every move and had to be wondering why she was leaving alone ten minutes after their arrival, Kathy endeavoured to look composed. Then suddenly, from the house behind her, she heard the unmistakable noise of glass smashing and splintering. The vintage wine bottle hitting the fireplace? Her narrow shoulders straightened, her chin came up. Eyes sparkling with satisfaction and with a new purpose in her step, she headed for the waiting car.

Over the next two weeks, however, Kathy grew steadily

more exhausted. Tigger died in his sleep without fuss or fanfare and she was inconsolable at the loss of her elderly pet. While she fretted about the future and grieved for her cat, her morning sickness spread to other times of day and she began lying awake at night worrying. Being pregnant and ill was more of a struggle than she had expected and she had to cut back on her hours at the café. Aware that Kathy was already struggling to pay her bills, Bridget offered Kathy her spare room, but Kathy was determined not to take advantage of their friendship.

Kathy would have vehemently protested any suggestion that she was waiting for Sergio to make another move. But when she discovered that Sergio was fully engaged in making moves that had nothing to do with her whatsoever, she had a rather rude awakening to reality. Travelling into work on the bus, she caught an infuriating flash of Sergio's face on a newspaper page. She wasn't close enough to see what the article was about and, while she told herself that she shouldn't care, she was only human. As soon as she got off the bus she bought the tabloid and paid the price for her curiosity.

Sergio, she learned, was the owner of a giant yacht called *Diva Queen* and he had thrown a stag party on board for his friend, Leonidas Pallis, the Greek billionaire. An exotic dancer talked of a 'non-stop orgy on the high seas.' Kathy studied the grainy photo of Sergio, shirt hanging open, engaging in dirty dancing with a pneumatic semi-naked blonde. Even drunk and carousing he still looked gorgeous and she swallowed hard. He really did like blondes, she thought dully. He also looked as if he was having fun. No doubt it beat the hell out of chess.

This was not a guy any woman would choose to have

an unplanned baby with, Kathy acknowledged heavily. Yet, how could she fault him when he had already accepted responsibility and was ready to help her financially? At no stage had he told her how he actually felt about the prospect of becoming a father and now she realised that he didn't need to tell her when his behaviour spoke so clearly for him. He was trying to ship her off to France to live under an assumed name where their paths would only cross at his instigation. And Sergio's riotous partying was making headlines round the world, while prompting an anonymous source to admit surprise at the sheer scale of his recent bad-boy activities.

Kathy believed that Sergio was reacting to the situation he had found himself in. He didn't want to be a father and he was even less happy that the mother of his child was a convicted thief. Those were the unlovely facts and it was time she learned to live with them and matched his independence. A good first move would be sorting out her immediate future on her own, for at this stage of her pregnancy there was no need for Sergio to be involved. In any case, a cooling-off period would probably do them both the world of good, she reflected painfully. She needed time and space to make her mind up about what she wanted to do after the baby was born. Hanging around in the hope that Sergio Torrente would somehow provide an answer for all her doubts and fears was a sure path to disappointment.

That evening she ate with Bridget at her apartment and outlined her intentions. 'I'll have to leave London. If I stop working at the café I won't be able to make my rent,' she confided ruefully. 'And I don't want to depend on Sergio for help.'

'Why not?'

Kathy dug into her tote bag and passed the newspaper across the table.

Bridget perused the article, raised her brows and set it aside without comment. 'If you don't mind kids and cooking, you can go to my god-daughter in Devon,' she said abruptly.

'Your god-daughter?' Kathy repeated with a frown. 'The estate agent?'

'Nola's energetic and practical just like you. You'll like each other. Her husband's a journalist and hardly ever at home. She's heavily pregnant with her fourth child and desperate for help,' the other woman said. 'Her nanny got married, and in the past two months two au pairs have come and gone. The first was so homesick she couldn't stop crying and the second quit because the house was too far out of town. What do you think?'

'I'll consider any option,' Kathy answered. 'There's nothing to keep me here.'

CHAPTER SEVEN

KATHY had just walked into the estate agency where Nola worked when the first pain hit.

With a muffled gasp, she clutched the edge of a desk to steady herself. The fear that engulfed her was much worse than the slight cramping sensation that gripped her lower abdomen.

'What's wrong?' Nola demanded, breaking off her conversation with another employee.

'I think the baby's coming!' Kathy whispered shakily, white as the wall behind her. 'But it's too soon.'

Nola Ross, a sensible brown-eyed blonde in her thirties, pressed Kathy down into a chair. 'Breathe in and out slowly. It may just be a Braxton-Hicks contraction.'

But the pains kept on coming and the two women decided that Kathy should go to the local hospital. There, Kathy insisted that Nola went back to the agency because she knew that the other woman had clients to meet. The doctor gave Kathy medication in an effort to stop the contractions and made arrangements to have her transferred to a facility with a neonatal unit. By that stage several hours had passed. As there was no bed free, she was kept on a trolley while she waited for the transportation to arrive.

Lying there, Kathy prayed and struggled to keep panic at bay. She was only thirty-five weeks pregnant and knew that her little girl would be at risk if she was born too early. The past seven months seemed to run on fast forward through Kathy's mind. She had not worked as Nola's domestic support for very long. No sooner had Nola had her own baby than her husband had taken off with another woman, plunging the Ross family into chaos. During that testing time, Nola and Kathy had become firm friends. By now Kathy had recovered from her early pregnancy sickness and helped out at the estate agency while Nola was briefly on maternity leave. She'd discovered that she was a whizz at selling houses! It was now three months since Nola had engaged a full-time nanny and hired Kathy as a saleswoman instead. In every way that mattered, Kathy's move from London to a small market town in Devon had proved an unqualified success.

But now Kathy was fast sinking into a pit of dread and self-blame. Determined to establish a secure base for herself and her child, she had worked hard because a career with prospects was the best possible safety net for a single parent. But had she worked too hard? Stressed too much? Rested too little? Once those preliminary bouts of nausea had melted away, she had felt amazingly healthy. Slowly but surely, her unborn baby had become the most important element of her world. The discovery that she was having a little girl had simply intensified her feelings. It had never once occurred to Kathy that her own body might let her down.

'Kathy…?'

As she recognised that unforgettable dark-timbred drawl shock flooded Kathy's taut length. She turned her head on the thin pillow, her apple-green gaze alight with astonishment. Sergio Torrente was poised several feet away just staring at her with sombre dark-as-night eyes.

'Are you okay?' he breathed tautly.

'No…' She squeezed out the word and it got tangled up in her vocal cords, and the next thing she knew she was sobbing as though her heart would break. In recent months, rigid self-discipline had prevented her from giving way too often to unproductive thoughts. His actual presence, however, was much more challenging at a moment when her defences were down and her emotions were out of her control. 'Go a-away!' she told him chokily.

In answer, Sergio made an unexpected move that had all the hallmarks of spontaneity. He smoothed her tangled hair off her damp brow and gripped her trembling hand in his. 'I can't leave you alone. Don't ask me to do that again.'

Kathy made use of the hanky he had produced for her use. 'How did you find out I was here?'

'Right now that's not important. I've already talked to the doctor. No doubt the staff has done their best, but you are lying unattended on a trolley in a corridor,' Sergio murmured in a wrathful undertone. 'That is not an acceptable level of care.'

'It's a small hospital and there's nothing more they can do for me at present,' Kathy mumbled unsteadily.

His hold on her fingers tightened. 'I have an air ambulance on its way and an obstetrician waiting to take charge. Please let me help.'

Kathy did not even have to think about how to respond to that offer, because in terms of treatment it was superior to anything else immediately available to her. Her spirits also received an immediate boost from the obvious fact that he placed as much importance on the safe birth of their child as she did. 'All right.'

His lean, darkly handsome features were tense and he made no attempt to hide his surprise. 'I thought you'd make me sweat through every possible argument.'

'All I care about is what's best for my baby,' Kathy admitted tightly. 'At this moment our differences don't matter.'

Everything moved very quickly after that. Attended by paramedics, she was stretchered onto the air ambulance. For the first time in months, she found herself actually worrying about what she looked like and she couldn't get over how silly and superficial she was being. How could she waste energy worrying that her eyelids and her nose might be pink and swollen? Or wondering if her large tummy equalled Mount Everest while she was lying flat? At best, she knew she had to look tired and tousled like most heavily pregnant women after a more than usually trying day. Even Sergio was a touch less perfect than usual, she reasoned in desperation. He had loosened his silk tie, dishevelled his black hair with impatient fingers and a blue-black shadow of stubble was beginning to define his stubborn jaw line and strong, sensual mouth. But he still looked totally amazing to her.

Just then he frowned with concern, visually questioning her lingering appraisal.

Cheeks reddening, Kathy shook her head to indicate that there was nothing wrong and shut her eyes tight. But the image of the guy she loved stayed with her. She loved him to bits, hated his guts for all sorts of reasons, as well, but she was still as possessed by a bone-deep longing for him as a starving woman sighting life-giving food. She knew he was bad for her, knew too big a dose of him was dangerous, but he was in her blood and in her mind and, no matter how hard she tried, she couldn't shake free of his influence over her.

In what seemed to her a remarkably short space of time, and with impressive efficiency, she was transported to the opulent comfort of a private London hospital. There she was given an ultrasound scan.

'I'd like to stay,' Sergio said flatly.

An objection was brimming on her lips and a glimpse of his taut profile warned her that that was exactly the response he expected from her. She swallowed back her protest because he was doing everything within his power to help and excluding him yet again seemed unfair. As she steeled herself to have her tummy exposed another thought occurred to her and she tugged at the sleeve of his jacket to get his attention.

Sergio angled his arrogant dark head down to her.

'We're having a girl,' she whispered.

Fine ebony brows drawing together, Sergio lifted his head and stared at her before comprehension sank in. Suddenly and entirely unexpectedly, a smile curved his wide sculpted mouth.

When the procedure commenced, she realised that she need not have worried about baring her swollen belly because Sergio's fascination was wholly reserved for the images on screen. A shot of the baby's face made him marvel out loud in Italian and reach for her hand. 'Awesome,' he finally murmured in roughened English. 'She is awesome.'

Tears dampened her eyes and she blinked them back fiercely. Some tests were carried out and a foetal monitor was attached to her, before she was finally slotted into bed in a luxurious private room. The obstetrician soothed her worst fears by telling her that babies born after the thirty-fourth week of gestation had a high rate of survival and less chance of suffering long-term complications. Even so, there were no guarantees and the longer her baby stayed in the womb the healthier she was likely to be. With Kathy still at risk of going into labour, the treatment plan was bed-rest and hydration.

Minutes after leaving with the obstetrician, Sergio reappeared.

'I thought you'd gone,' Kathy commented.

'*Per meraviglia*…I hope that's a joke.' Astute dark-as-night eyes rested on her. 'But it's not a joke, is it?'

Kathy sidestepped that issue, for she had not intended to annoy him. 'Well, now that we're on our own, at last you can tell me how long you've known where I was living.'

'I found out today at the same time as I heard you had been hospitalised.' Lean bronzed features bleak, Sergio studied her from the foot of the bed. 'I was last in the chain. Nola—whoever she is—contacted Bridget Kirk, who decided to pass the news on to Renzo Catallone.'

'Bridget told Renzo?' Her brows pleated in surprise. 'I didn't even know they'd met.'

'They've met all right. Evidently your friend is good at keeping secrets. When I spoke to her months ago, she swore that she had no idea where you were.'

Kathy was very much disconcerted. 'She didn't tell me you'd contacted her, either.'

'Renzo kept in touch with her and finally it paid off. But he also believed that she didn't know where you had gone.'

'I'm surprised that Bridget chose to tell Renzo.'

'Are you? With you on the brink of giving birth or possibly even losing my child, it was time to stop playing games.'

Kathy registered the cold core of his anger. The very fact that he was struggling to hide it, that his diamond-hard façade was no longer impregnable, warned her how deep his hostility had gone. 'Bridget was only respecting my wishes and trying to protect me—'

'From me?' Sergio sent her an almost raw glance and strode over to the window, his broad shoulders radiating his ferocious tension, before he swung back to look at her. 'Do I deserve that? Did I frighten you in any way?'

'No,' Kathy conceded.

'Perhaps something I did upset you…'

The verdant green eyes resting on him veiled. 'You're fishing.'

'I need to know. I don't want you pulling another vanishing act,' Sergio traded in a direct challenge.

Kathy contemplated the swollen mound of her tummy and opted for honesty. 'You asked for it.'

The silence fairly leapt and jumped and throbbed.

'Are you saying what I think you might be saying?' Sergio was studying her in disbelief. 'Was that a reference to the stag cruise I organised for Leonidas Pallis? That event was blown up out of all proportion by the press. But was that what upset you?'

'Lose the word, *upset*,' Kathy advised, a shade tart in tone.

His brilliant dark eyes shimmering scorching gold, Sergio spread lean brown hands in a gesture that expressed his incredulity. 'You were so angry about the cruise that you took off and put me through more than seven months of hell?'

'*Angry* isn't the right word, either—'

'How about…*revenge*?'

'I suppose there was a degree of that, although I didn't see it at the time,' Kathy conceded ruefully.

Sergio bit out a humourless laugh.

'I think I'd just had enough of you. I didn't want to be shipped off to France,' Kathy confided. 'There I was, throwing up every day and so tired I could hardly keep my eyes open at work and you were partying—'

'I can explain—'

'Don't waste your time. In any case you don't owe me any explanations,' Kathy fielded with resolute brightness. 'It's simple—I needed to get on with my life just the same as you were.'

Sergio dealt her a measuring appraisal. 'You don't just get mad, you get even, *delizia mia.*'

Kathy experienced a very strong desire to get out of bed and slap him for his arrogance. 'It's not all about you—why do you think everything is about you? Stop trying to twist what I said into a backhanded compliment! I had no good reason to stay in London.'

Lean, darkly handsome face taut, Sergio stared down at her with brooding force. 'You can't afford to get mad with me at present. You're supposed to stay calm and avoid all stress.'

In a frustrated movement, Kathy pushed her copper hair off her brow. 'Then rewind my life and wipe the bit where we met!'

'Even if I could I would not,' Sergio admitted without hesitation. 'I want that little girl. I also want you.'

Kathy was hugely unimpressed by that claim. Her green eyes glinted, her full rose-pink mouth curled with disdain. She was very tempted to tell him that the boat had not only sailed, but also sunk with all hands on board. He hadn't wanted her enough when it had mattered. He hadn't wanted her enough when she had been as available as a free sample. She said nothing, though, for telling him that would only make her sound sad.

'And whatever it takes, I intend to have you,' Sergio delivered in the same even tone.

Kathy blinked, for she was not quite sure she had heard that. Her curling lashes lifted high. She collided with the hot gold challenge of his gaze and it was like being hauled down into a whirlpool of heat and hunger. He made no attempt to hide the desire etched on his lean strong face and sheer shock paralysed her to the bed.

'Okay. Glad we understand each other at last, *delizia mia*,' Sergio murmured smooth as silk as he pressed the bell on the wall. 'I asked for a meal to be brought and I'd like you to try to eat something.'

But when the meal arrived, Kathy was unable to oblige for she had no appetite at all. Sergio took a seat at the far end of the room and unfurled a notebook PC with a disturbing air of permanency, while she lay on the side she had been told to lie on and fretted. Why was it that every time she got her life back on track something happened to derail it again? She reminded herself that she had played a very active part in this particular derailment.

Frustration filled her at the awareness that the dependency she had been so determined to avoid was now being forced on her. Lying in bed in London wasn't going to pay her bills. If her baby was born early and in need of specialist care, she would be even more dependent on Sergio's goodwill and support to survive. She had planned to work right up to the last minute. How long would she be tied to London? For how long could she expect Nola to hold her job open? What about her rent? Her possessions?

'Why are you frowning?' Sergio enquired lazily.

'Promise me that if I'm stuck in here for weeks, you'll collect my belongings and keep them safe for me,' Kathy urged abruptly.

With a wondering shake of his handsome dark head, Sergio sprang upright and strolled with lithe grace towards the bed. 'What could possibly make you worry about something like that?'

'I'm not fit enough to take care of it myself and everything I own is at Nola's.'

'But why on earth would you imagine that it could become a problem?'

'When I was arrested four years ago, I lost everything I owned while I was in custody,' Kathy admitted tightly. 'Family photos, keepsakes, clothes, *everything*. I don't want it to happen again and it could so easily.'

Sergio frowned. 'How did that happen?'

'There was nobody to take responsibility for my things while I was in prison, so what I owned was either dumped or sold. Gareth promised that he would store my stuff for me, but then he let his mother ditch me and I never heard from him again—'

'His mother?' Sergio studied her in astonishment.

'She visited me in prison to tell me that her son was finished with me. I wrote to him and my landlady, but neither of them bothered to reply.'

'I'll have your possessions collected for you the moment you say the word. Believe me, you won't lose a single item.' Lean brown fingers curling to the footboard on the bed, Sergio surveyed her with disturbingly intent dark eyes. 'We share a mutual distrust of our fellow man. How can I prove to you that although I have my faults you can trust my word?'

'You can't.' Kathy was tense because she was experiencing a tightening sensation that she was afraid might be the forerunner of the contractions that had faded away some hours earlier.

'Even if I ask you to marry me?'

Her heart gave a slow, heavy thud and she stared at him fixedly. 'Are you asking?'

'Yes, *bellezza mia*.' Sergio met her startled appraisal with rock-solid calm. 'You're having my baby. It's the most rational solution.'

'But people don't get married just because—'

'In my family they do,' Sergio cut in.

Kathy contemplated the armchair he had vacated. She didn't want to snatch at his offer and give his ego an unnecessary boost. If she considered his proposal purely in terms of security and common sense, however, it answered her every practical need, for she would no longer need to worry about how she would manage as a mother. Indeed if she married Sergio the luxury of choice would enter her world again and her little girl would never have to make the sacrifices her mother had. Her adoptive parents had instilled enough of their principles to ensure that marriage had much more appeal for Kathy than the worry of having to go it alone with her child. If he was willing to commit to that extent to their daughter's future, she reckoned that he was much more responsible and reliable than she had given him credit for.

Kathy tried not to grimace as the sensation in her abdomen became definite enough to warn her that she was going into labour again. It was a very vulnerable moment and she fully recognised the fact. He didn't love her, but he was willing to be there for her as the father of her child. Just then that mattered to her as much as the knowledge that if she said yes, he would stay with her.

'Okay…I'll marry you,' she muttered jerkily.

'I'll organise it.' His lean dark features serious, Sergio's smooth response bore the infuriating hallmarks of a male who had not expected any other reply. 'We'll organise the ceremony before the baby's born—'

'I don't th-think so,' Kathy gasped as another pain rippled in a wave across her lower body, returning stronger and faster than she had expected. 'My contractions have started again. Our baby's going to get here first.'

Momentarily, Sergio dealt her a look of consternation, but then he unfroze and wasted no time in summoning assistance. Events moved fast from that point. Both of them were filled with dismay when the surgeon decided that a Caesarean section would be the safest, speediest option for the delivery. Kathy was frightened for her child and Sergio made an enormous effort to keep her calm. His strength and assurance helped her a great deal. Clad in green theatre scrubs, he held her hand throughout the procedure and talked her through every step. He looked very pale but the delivery went without a hitch. Only in the instant after Sergio first saw their daughter did Kathy fully appreciate how much of a front he could put up, and that his anxiety had been equal to her own, for his stunning dark deep-set eyes were lustrous with tears.

Their newborn infant was checked over with great care. She had slight breathing problems, so was immediately placed in an incubator and whisked away.

Kathy was returned to her room. 'I'd like to call our

daughter Ella after my mother,' she said tautly, keen to personalise their child with a name, so that even if she couldn't hold the tiny girl at that moment she could feel closer to her.

'Ella Battista…after mine,' Sergio suggested.

The effects of stress, exhaustion and medication were steadily piling up on Kathy and making her eyes very heavy. Sergio went to check on Ella and came back to report on her progress before Kathy finally let herself fall asleep.

Nola Ross phoned the next morning and sent flowers. Bridget arrived and joined Kathy in the special care baby unit, where quite some time was spent admiring Ella with her silky fluff of coppery curls and fine features. 'Are you annoyed with me for getting Sergio involved?' Bridget asked worriedly, once Kathy had been conveyed back to her room and the two women had the privacy to talk.

Kathy was grateful to be distracted from her ever-present worry about her baby's health. 'Of course I'm not. But why didn't you mention Sergio's visit or Renzo's?'

Bridget winced. 'I knew it would stress you out if you realised that Sergio was making a big push to find you, and then things got really complicated…'

'How?'

'Don't mention it to Sergio yet, but I'm dating Renzo.'

Kathy gave her a bemused look, and then she began to laugh. The brunette made Kathy smile with her story of how the middle-aged Italian's regular visits to the café had led to a friendship that had warmed into something more serious.

'I'd pretended I didn't know where you were at first. Then I had to keep up the pretence because Renzo was too loyal to Sergio to be trusted with the truth—'

'You should have told me.'

'You had enough on your plate. To be fair to Sergio, the guy hasn't stopped looking for you since you left London.'

'Guilty conscience. I should've left him a note telling him not to worry and that I'd be fine,' Kathy conceded wryly.

'But the dramatic silence and the walk-out was much more your style, *bellezza mia*,' Sergio interposed from the doorway. 'Mrs Kirk...I hope Kathy has invited you to our wedding.'

The older woman's eyes expanded like saucers. 'What wedding?' she exclaimed. 'You two are planning to get married? That is wonderful news!'

'I hadn't got around to mentioning it yet.' Beneath Sergio's sardonic appraisal, Kathy squirmed and flushed. She had found it impossible to find the right words with which to make that announcement when deep down inside she felt as though agreeing to marry him was a betrayal of her principles and her pride. 'It won't be for ages yet anyway,' she added. 'I mean, we'll have to wait until Ella's strong enough to leave the baby unit and I've recovered from the Caesarean.'

In actuality, Ella finally gained her release from medical care only three days before her parents were due to marry and, by then, she was seven weeks old. The little girl had overcome the breathing problems caused by her under-developed lungs only to be diagnosed with anaemia. At one stage, a worrying infection had kept Kathy at the hospital with her daughter day and night. With a vast business empire demanding his attention, Sergio had been unable to be on the spot as often, but he had shared every crisis with Kathy and his daughter. It was Sergio's strength that Kathy had learnt to rely on at the lowest moments. His courage in the face of adversity and his refusal to contemplate a negative outcome had grounded Kathy and given her hope when she had been most afraid for their child. Once the danger passed, however, Sergio had gone back abroad.

He had suggested that Kathy move into his apartment, but a suite in the quiet hotel across the road from the hospital had proved to be more convenient and she had seen no reason to move out before the wedding. That physical separation, allied to the need to concentrate solely on Ella's problems, had created a polite distance between Sergio and Kathy. In addition, Sergio had been determined to keep the press from finding out about Ella and his marital plans before he chose to make an official announcement. As a result their meetings had acquired a level of discretion that had ensured that they invariably only saw each other at the hospital. And there they had been virtually never alone.

Although Sergio had belatedly attempted to break the stalemate, Kathy had made endless excuses about needing to stay with Ella or being too tired while she recovered from her op. Kathy was miserably convinced that all the secrecy was aimed at keeping her shameful past hidden for as long as possible. So, how could Sergio really want to risk being seen out with her in public? Wouldn't it only hasten her exposure as a convicted thief? The paparazzi followed Sergio's every move with intense interest. Kathy reckoned that about five minutes after she was revealed as the new Mrs Torrente her criminal record would be dug up and paraded in newsprint for all to see. The very thought of it made her feel sick with dread. But worst of all was the knowledge that Sergio would also feel that humiliation—and that some day her daughter would, as well.

In the background, the wedding arrangements had been handled by experts who worked in tandem with Sergio's staff. Italy had been chosen as the ideal location and every detail had been kept under wraps. Kathy only had Bridget and Nola on her guest list, and her friends were over the moon at the prospect of a luxury weekend in the sunshine. The one item that Kathy had chosen for herself was her wedding gown.

Forty-eight hours before the wedding, the hotel reception called Kathy's suite to inform her that Mr Torrente was on his way up to see her. Surprised because she had not expected to see Sergio before she flew out to Italy with her friends the next day, Kathy stopped packing Ella's clothes and rushed to check her hair instead. She was astonished when she opened the door to a stranger, because the stringent security precautions Sergio insisted on meant that nobody she didn't know should even get as far as the lift.

A portly man with receding hair and rather sad brown eyes smiled at her. 'I'm Abramo Torrente, Sergio's brother.'

'My goodness…' Kathy had the tact not to say that she had quite forgotten that her bridegroom even had a brother. 'Please come in.'

'You should check my credentials first.' Abramo extended his passport as evidence of his identity. 'You can't be too careful nowadays.'

Certainly the brothers bore little resemblance to each other. Abramo looked more cuddly than sexy and, where Sergio was in the physical peak of condition the younger man had a grey indoor pallor. She had to strain her memory to recall that Sergio was the child of his father's first marriage and Abramo the child of the second.

'My brother hasn't told you anything about me, has he?'

Abramo, Kathy registered, was shrewder than he seemed at first glance. 'I'm afraid not.'

'It's eight years since Sergio spoke to me. He refuses to see me. He's an old-world Torrente in the style of our late father—stubborn and hard as iron,' Abramo commented heavily. 'But we are still brothers.'

'Eight years is a long time. It must have been some family feud.'

'Sergio was the innocent victim of my mother's lies,' Abramo admitted ruefully. 'My father favoured him and she resented that. I loved my brother but I envied him too. Once I saw how Sergio's fall might give me a chance with Grazia, I was no better than my mother. I stood by and did nothing to help him regain what was rightfully his.'

'Grazia?' Kathy prompted in fascination. 'Who's Grazia?'

'Surely Sergio has mentioned her to you?'

'No.'

Abramo contrived to look stunned by that oversight. 'When Sergio was twenty-one he got engaged to Grazia. I too loved her,' he confided with a grimace. 'When Sergio was deposed as heir to the Azzarini wine empire and I took his place, Grazia panicked and changed her mind about marrying him. I didn't waste the opportunity. I married her before she could change her mind.'

Kathy marvelled at his honesty and at his evident hope that Sergio would absolve him from what must have been a devastating double betrayal. 'I'm not sure I understand why you're telling me all this.'

'Sergio is about to marry you. You have a child. All our lives are in a different place now. I want to offer my good wishes for your future. I have a great need to make peace with my brother.' Abramo gave her a look of unashamed appeal. 'Will you speak to him?'

Ella wakened in the room next door and her cries created

a welcome diversion. Kathy lifted her tiny precious daughter from her cradle and hugged her gently close. Family ties were important, she reflected helplessly. Although Abramo's sincerity had impressed her, she was reluctant to interfere in a situation about which she knew so little. She took Ella out to meet her uncle. He was one of those men who absolutely adored babies and was enchanted with his niece. Kathy was surprised to learn that he had no children of his own.

'I'll have a word with Sergio after the wedding,' Kathy said finally. 'But that's all I can promise.'

Abramo gripped her hands in a warmly enthusiastic expression of gratitude and swore she would not regret it. As soon as he had left, Kathy made use of the internet and did a search for Grazia Torrente. A startling number of websites came up: Grazia was a celebrity in mainland Europe, the fashionista daughter of an Italian marquis with an alarmingly long name. Up came a picture of an ethereal blonde with the face of a Madonna and a figure that would make even a sack look trendy. As couples went, Abramo and Grazia matched like oil and water, whereas Sergio and…Her face tight with discomfiture, Kathy closed the page and scolded herself for snooping. After all, it was *eight* years since he had been engaged to the woman who was now married to his brother.

That night the cheerful nanny whom Kathy had picked from a short list arrived to help with Ella. The next day, they departed for the airport, where they met up with Bridget and Nola. Ten minutes later, Kathy's mobile phone rang.

'I hear you're having a good time,' Sergio murmured teasingly.

Kathy stiffened. 'Have you got your security team spying on me now?'

'No need, *delizia mia*. I can hear the giggles from where I'm standing and it sounds very much like a hen-party.'

'From where you're standing?' Kathy froze and looked up. Her searching gaze fanned round before it homed straight in on Sergio's unmistakable tall, well-built frame. Sun shades in place, he was talking on his phone about fifty yards away. 'I didn't know you were here—'

'No, don't come over. Ignore me,' Sergio urged as she began to rise from her seat. 'We're travelling separately. You're flying to Italy in a Pallis jet to keep the paparazzi off our trail.'

'Is your friend Leonidas throwing in male strippers to enliven our flight?' Her apple-green eyes were bright as danger flares. 'Maybe I want to do more than have a giggle over a cup of coffee during my last hours as a single woman.'

Across the concourse, Sergio raised lean brown fingers to his lips and blew on them as though he had been burnt. 'You are never going to let me forget that stag cruise, are you?'

Chin at an angle, Kathy lifted and dropped a slim shoulder in an exaggerated shrug. 'What do you think?'

'I think that christening my yacht *Diva Queen* was an act of prophecy, *delizia mia*,' Sergio drawled. 'By the way, be nice about Leonidas. He and his wife are hosting our wedding…'

CHAPTER EIGHT

A COURTEOUS steward escorted Kathy and her party onto the Pallis jet.

Kathy was surprised to find two women waiting on board to greet them. A shapely chestnut-haired girl with violet eyes and a ready smile introduced herself as Maribel Pallis and her stunning blonde companion as Tilda, Princess Hussein Al-Zafar. They were the wives of Sergio's friends from his university days, Leonidas and Rashad.

'The guys are like this…' Tilda meshed her fingers together in a speaking gesture to explain the strength of the men's friendship. 'We couldn't wait until you got to Italy to meet you.'

'I always thought it would take a big game hunter to land Sergio,' Maribel teased.

Kathy resisted the urge to comment that a six-pound baby had accomplished that feat all on her own and without the use of a weapon. It might be the truth, she thought heavily, but it would also be a conversational killer when Tilda and Maribel were making a wonderful effort to extend a friendly welcome. Then Ella opened her baby version of her mother's unusual light green eyes to inspect their new acquaintances and any remaining barriers fell, for every woman present was a mother and there was plenty of common ground to share. That led into Maribel asking soon after takeoff if there was any chance that Kathy fancied a night out rather than a sedate pre-bridal early night.

Kathy gave Maribel a look of surprise. 'Any sort of a night out would be a thrill,' she confided ruefully. 'I stayed in while I was pregnant and after the birth I was tied to the hospital until last week.'

Tilda and Maribel exchanged smiles. 'Let's go for the thrill.'

'Sergio always does.' Kathy spoke her thoughts out loud and then blushed at that revealing comment, which her companions were too tactful to pick up on.

When the jet landed in Tuscany, Ella and her nanny were borne off to the Pallis country estate while Kathy and her companions headed into the medieval splendour of Florence for a whirlwind shopping trip. There Kathy finally got to make use of the credit cards Sergio had given her and that breathless, chattering tour of exclusive boutiques was a lot of fun. It soon transpired that the night out was a pre-planned event that had merely required her approval. The five women enjoyed the comfort of a luxury hotel suite as a changing room and sashayed out to dinner in style.

Maribel took a picture of Kathy with her phone. Kathy's new turquoise dress was a fabulous foil for her colouring and very long legs. 'One for the album, I think.'

Within five minutes of that picture being taken, Kathy's mobile phone rang. It was Sergio. 'I couldn't believe it when Ella arrived without you. Where are you?'

'Enjoying dinner. I'm having a hen-night,' Kathy told him chirpily.

'It feels like you've been kidnapped. I don't know what

Maribel and Tilda are playing at, but it's inappropriate to stage that kind of event this close to our wedding,' Sergio informed her with censorious cool.

Chagrined colour surged into Kathy's cheeks and she excused herself from her companions to move to a more private area where she could speak without being overheard. 'I wasn't aware that I asked for your opinion!'

'My opinion comes free of charge. You have to be exhausted; you've only just recovered from your delivery. Just tell me where you are. I'll come and collect you,' Sergio responded, his hard shell of self-assurance impervious to her furious response.

'Forget it! Wouldn't that be a great way to thank Maribel for her kindness in organising entertainment for me?'

'Is that why Maribel sent me a photo of you in a very short dress? And told me not to wait up for you because you were going clubbing?' Sergio queried, unimpressed. 'My take on this would be that this is payback time for the stag cruise I organised for Leonidas—'

'Well, even if it is, you can be sure that we'll be doing something more fun and more intelligent than getting off our faces on booze and carousing with half-naked dancers!' Kathy blazed down the phone in an incandescent rage before she cut the connection. 'You know why? We've got more class and imagination!'

As Kathy stalked back across the restaurant her phone pulsed and lit up. She switched it off quickly and thrust it into her bag. He was so incredibly bossy. Did he think she was a feckless teenager in need of a curfew?

'Was that Sergio on the phone?' Bridget enquired.

'He wants us to have a brilliant time!' Kathy fibbed with a set smile.

The women entered the nightclub by a rear entrance where they were welcomed by the management team. Flanked by a platoon of security guards, they were swept into an interior extravagantly modelled on a Moroccan Kasbah with exotic lights and very private seating areas embellished by colourful silks and fat cushioned divans.

Kathy was coming off the dance floor with Nola when a tiny curvaceous blonde in an eye catching white short suit intercepted her. 'I'm Grazia Torrente,' she announced. 'Abramo's wife.'

A bemused smile crossed Kathy's expressive mouth, because she had not appreciated that Grazia would be so much smaller than she was. Nola excused herself and returned to their party.

'I've been dying to meet you ever since I heard about you. Come and sit down with me.' Grazia linked arms with Kathy in an intimate fashion and made it quite impossible for her to walk away again without administering a pointed snub.

Kathy disliked the lack of choice extended to her, but natural curiosity about Sergio's former fiancée won. 'How did you know who I was?'

Languorous turquoise-blue eyes rested on her and the chill there sent a frisson of unease darting through Kathy. 'You're out on the town with an army of bodyguards in the company of Maribel Pallis and the Crown Princess of Bakhar? Who else could you be but Sergio's bride? As to how I found you, I have connections.'

'I'm sure you do and it would be lovely to sit and chat, but I can't leave my party for long. We're leaving soon,' Kathy responded.

'Sergio is only using you to punish me, Kathy.' The tiny blonde's turquoise eyes were bold and sharp as knives, her voice full of soft scorn. 'He's not a forgiving man. I let him down when I married his loser brother and now I have to pay the price and watch him marry you. It really is that simple—an almost biblical act of revenge. Only when Sergio decides that I've suffered enough will he snap his fingers and allow me back into his life on a permanent basis.'

Flushed and taut, Kathy studied Grazia, whose perfect features were framed by silken wings of silvery blonde hair. The other woman was even more beautiful than she had looked in pictures. 'I think you're the one with the problem. Maybe you never got over Sergio—'

Grazia vented a sarcastic laugh. 'I'm warning you. You're way out of your comfort zone—a clueless little English girl with no idea how a complex man like Sergio operates. You're caught up in something that has nothing to do with you and you can't win because I will *always* be the girl he idolised at eighteen.'

'For goodness' sake, you're married to his brother!' Kathy breathed in reproof, losing patience with the blonde's drama and standing up to leave.

'I'm in the process of divorcing Abramo—as Sergio told me to do,' Grazia declared with a pitying smile. 'Don't be fooled. Sergio may act like he despises me, but he is still determined to have me. So, he's marrying you to give his daughter his name, just like his father did a generation ago for Abramo. But what's a ring on those terms worth? A comfortable divorce settlement? Sergio can afford it.'

Kathy walked away feeling hollow with uncertainty and angry that she had even listened. But the news that Grazia and Abramo were divorcing had come as a shock. Even so, she reasoned, that did not necessarily mean that there was an ongoing connection of any kind between Grazia and

Sergio. Her temples were tight with tension. She lifted her hand to massage the taut skin. Maribel suggested that perhaps it was time to call it a night. Bridget asked Kathy if she was tired and she admitted that she was.

Grazia told a good story, Kathy acknowledged unhappily. Sergio had enough powerful pride, ferocious strength of will and a dark, deep secretive nature to nourish the concept of revenge. He kept his emotions in a private place. And nobody knew better than Kathy how closely love, hate and sexual hunger could interconnect until it was impossible to define the boundaries. Grazia did indeed have terrific connections, since not only had she known where to find Kathy that evening, but she was also one of the select few who knew about Ella's existence.

Leonidas and Maribel Pallis owned a huge country house outside Siena. Kathy scrambled out of the car, eager to see Sergio even if it meant a confrontation. But there was no sign of the men. Maribel took Kathy to the nursery to see Ella, who was sleeping soundly in her cradle. Kathy was then shown into the superb private suite set aside for the bride's use and left alone. Feeling incredibly weary and free to finally show it, Kathy simply sagged like a worn rag doll. Even the thought of getting undressed was a challenge.

The door opened and she jumped. A tall dark male appeared on the threshold and her heart pounded like a road drill in an instant leap of pleasure and relief.

'I won't say I told you so,' Sergio murmured lazily.

Her attention closed in and clung to him. He was the image of natural elegance in a well-cut jacket and designer jeans. She stamped down hard on an anxious thought about Grazia, determined not to panic into asking stupid questions that would only create friction. 'About what?

'Maribel and Tilda have no idea how exhausted you are, *delizia mia*. You had a difficult birth and weeks of round-the-clock worry about Ella, and it will take time for you to get over that.'

Guilt assailed Kathy, for when he had phoned her earlier she had assumed that he was objecting to her going out on the town when it was obvious that concern had motivated him. 'I could've said no to the night out.'

'How often do you go for the sensible option around me?'

A dulled flush of chagrin lit Kathy's drawn features, for it was true. She was so vigilant in fighting her own corner that her choices often related more to a statement of independence than practicality. He moved forward and lifted her up into his arms with easy strength to carry her through to the bedroom where he set her down on the bed. She fought an urgent desire to touch the arrogant dark head momentarily level with her knees as he bent to tug off her shoes. She wanted him to stay; she wanted him to stay so badly she dug her hands like talons into the bedspread. But she said nothing because she was determined not to be a clingy, needy woman.

'You need all the rest you can get for the wedding.' In the act of straightening, Sergio paused to swoop down on her ripe pink mouth and claim it in a kiss that startled her and rocked her with a pleasure that made her pulses race. 'And for me, *dolcezza mia*.'

She lay in bed in the darkness drowsily reliving that erotic thrill. At the same time she was ashamed of herself for not telling him about Abramo's visit or Grazia's poisonous forecast. Keeping secrets from the guy she was about to marry didn't feel right. On the other hand, if she wasn't careful he might think she was the jealous type, liable to turn into a bunny boiler. She was painfully aware that he didn't love her and was only prepared to marry her for Ella's benefit. What if a reference to Grazia sparked off a change of heart on his part? Kathy despised herself for being so fearful. When had Sergio become so precious to her that the prospect of life without him loomed like a death sentence?

Kathy was truly enjoying her wedding day.

Maribel's efficient planning had ensured that everything ran like clockwork, from the moment Kathy wakened to a delicious breakfast in bed to the arrival of a parade of beauticians eager to groom the bride to perfection. The pure white off-the-shoulder dress clung to her delicate curves and small waist before flaring out into a full skirt and a swirling embroidered train worthy of a royal wedding. The gown was rather more adaptable, however, than its traditional style suggested.

Mid-morning, Kathy employed reverent fingers to examine the magnificent jewellery that had been brought to her. It had arrived complete with a note from Sergio asking her to wear the emerald and pearl suite worn by generations of Torrente brides. Kathy slowly shook her head in wonderment. 'I'll glitter like a Christmas tree.'

'Who wouldn't like the problem?' Bridget quipped.

'It will look amazing. That's a spectacular set and your dress is plain enough to carry it,' Nola opined.

The church was an ancient medieval building shaded by massive trees on the slopes of a sleepy hill village. When Bridget and Nola assisted Kathy from the limo, Sergio was waiting outside to give Kathy a glorious bouquet. As Sergio descended the steps the bridal couple were so busily engaged in looking at each other that in the exchange the flowers almost fell to the ground.

'I like the dress,' Sergio breathed tautly.

Kathy collided with his dark deep-set eyes. Lean, strong features serious, he was so dazzlingly handsome and so achingly familiar that she felt almost dizzy with delight. She didn't even notice Bridget putting out a hand to steady her hold on the flowers. Moving into the dim cool of the church with the heady scent of roses heavy on the still air and the magic musical notes of a harp swelling to greet them, Kathy was conscious only of Sergio.

An interpreter translated every word of the lengthy service for her benefit. Every word had meaning for her and she could feel a kind of peace stealing over her: her life and her future seemed more promising to her than it had in a very long time. She wanted to believe that the dark times were over. She had her precious little daughter and now she was marrying the man that she loved. Just at that moment she refused to qualify those beliefs with a single negative connotation.

Walking down the aisle on Sergio's arm and out into the sunshine, Kathy was radiant. 'How do you feel?' she asked him.

'Grateful it's over,' Sergio murmured with all the off-the-cuff immediacy of serious sincerity. 'I don't like weddings, *dolcezza mia*.'

That sobering little speech engulfed Kathy like an unexpected deluge of cold water. It made her feel foolish and naïve. It knocked her right off her fluffy bridal cloud of contentment and back down to earth again. 'It's going to be a long day for you, then. Leonidas and Maribel are really pushing out the boat for us.'

Sergio laughed softly as he lifted Kathy into the wonderful fairy-tale flower-bedecked carriage awaiting them. 'Maribel knows how I feel about weddings. She has a terrific sense of humour and she's making the most of the opportunity.'

His irreverent attitude did nothing to raise her spirits. Drinks were served back at the imposing house where many more guests were arriving. Innumerable introductions followed and when the swamp of people seeking them became too pressing, Sergio swept her off to take a seat at the top table in the magnificent ballroom. Kathy paused only to remove the detachable train from her gown. She laughed in appreciation when she saw that the wedding décor was based on a chess motif with witty touches—that idea could only have originated with Sergio. She was pleased that he had had the interest to make that choice.

After the two best men, Leonidas and Prince Rashad had made brief and amusing speeches, Bridget said just a few words in which she described Kathy as the daughter of her heart. As she spoke the two women exchanged a look of warm affection and Sergio later asked his bride when she had first met the older woman.

Kathy tensed. 'I don't think you want to know.'

'You're my wife,' Sergio said levelly. 'There's nothing you can't tell me.'

Kathy resisted the urge to remind him that he had refused to listen when she had told him that she wasn't a thief. She was all too well aware that plenty of other people would share his scepticism.

'Bridget's daughter died in custody ten years ago. She took her own life,' Kathy told him in a hesitant undertone. 'Ever since then, Bridget has volunteered as a prison visitor. We met when I was in hospital in the second year of my sentence. She's a wonderful woman and she became my lifeline.'

Sergio closed a lean masculine hand over her slim fingers, which she was involuntarily clenching and unclenching on her lap in an unconscious betrayal of tension. 'I'm grateful she was there for you, *dolcezza mia*.'

After the meal, Kathy went off to freshen up. It was time to allow her highly adaptable wedding gown to enter its final reinvention. She removed the full constricting skirt of her dress to reveal a shorter, more fitted skirt and returned with Maribel to the ballroom in fashionable style. When he saw her, Sergio stilled in surprise and admiration before moving forward to greet her, brilliant dark eyes intent on her stunning face. He swept her out onto the floor to dance. 'You look spectacular in the family jewels.'

'So would most women.'

'But they wouldn't have your hair, your face or your astonishing legs, *bella mia*,' Sergio husked. 'You look gorgeous.'

Two hours later, Kathy came downstairs with Maribel after checking on Ella, who was sleeping soundly. Maribel and Tilda had put their children to bed, but not without some protest. Sharaf, Bethany and Elias had made a concerted and comical effort to push bedtime back another few minutes. With her green eyes sparkling and laughter still on her lips, Kathy was in the best of spirits when she returned to the ballroom. That mood took a sharp downturn at the same moment that she spotted the exquisite blonde seated at a table by the edge of the dance floor.

It was Grazia. At first Kathy couldn't believe the evidence of her own eyes. It didn't help that a whole host of people were also exhibiting surprise at the appearance of the bridegroom's one-time fiancée. Indeed, as Kathy watched with growing disbelief, Grazia responded to the attention with little nods and smiles and even lifted a hand in acknowledgement very much like visiting royalty. Evidently she was a late arrival.

'What's wrong?' Maribel Pallis asked, because Kathy had stopped dead and fallen silent.

'Was Grazia Torrente on Sergio's guest list?'

'I'll check.' Maribel signalled a staff member. 'Who is she? A relative?'

'She's still married to Sergio's brother, but Sergio used to be engaged to her,' Kathy framed shakily, high spots of colour beginning to bloom over her taut cheekbones. 'I can't believe she had the cheek to come to our wedding—'

'Are you sure you're not mistaking her for someone else?' Tilda prompted.

'No chance! Once met, never forgotten.'

Both women followed the path of Kathy's gaze and Maribel exclaimed, 'My goodness, isn't that the same woman who approached you at the club last night?'

Kathy shifted her hands in a hasty dismissive gesture. 'Don't worry about it, Maribel. I'm being silly.'

But that was only a polite plea for Maribel's benefit, because Kathy did not want to make her hostess feel that she was in any way responsible for Grazia's unwelcome appearance. No, Kathy knew exactly who she should be tackling on that score and she wasted no time in tracking down Sergio. She found him talking business in a secluded corner with Leonidas and Rashad.

Kathy headed for Sergio like a high-velocity bullet aimed at a target. 'Could we have a word?'

Leonidas Pallis gave her an amused appraisal. 'That sounds ominous.'

'I don't think so,' Sergio drawled, smooth as glass.

'Trust me,' the Greek tycoon urged his friend with lazy mockery. 'I've been married longer.'

'Leonidas,' Prince Rashad interposed on a wry note.

Sergio strolled back into the crowded ballroom by Kathy's side. 'Is there a problem?'

'Did you invite your ex-fiancée to our wedding?' Kathy questioned tautly.

Sergio stilled. 'Who are you referring to?'

Suspecting that he was deliberately sidestepping a direct answer to her query, Kathy lifted her coppery head high. 'Grazia! Who else?'

'I wasn't aware that you even knew she existed,' Sergio remarked in the most deflating tone.

Kathy folded her arms in a defensive movement and recalled how keen Grazia had been to ensure that Kathy knew exactly who she was. 'Oh, yes, I know all right. She's creating quite a stir.'

His lean, dark, handsome face cool and unrevealing, Sergio looked across the ballroom. Grazia was leaning back against a table flirting like mad with a bunch of young men, her aura of sensual allure a magnetic draw. Even in the middle of a crowd she was a high-profile presence who attracted attention. 'I'm afraid I don't know what the problem is.'

Kathy snatched in a deep jerky breath. She was so worked up that it was an effort. At that instant she could not even explain why she was getting so angry so quickly. All she knew was that Grazia's presence felt like a very public slap in the face. She felt humiliated and insecure and unnerved. She was now thinking that there might be a great deal more to Grazia's utterances than mere sour grapes. 'Don't you? She shouldn't be here. Why did you invite her?'

'I didn't,' Sergio murmured levelly. 'But she's with her cousin, who *was*. Perhaps he brought her as his guest.'

It was not a good moment for Kathy to be forced to appreciate that Grazia and her relations had an ongoing social entrée to his exclusive world. Inevitably that meant that a network of other connections could still link Sergio back to the beautiful blonde.

'I want her out of here,' Kathy confided and her voice shook because it was a struggle to keep her voice low in pitch.

'You're a Torrente now. That is not how we treat guests, welcome or otherwise.' Sardonic dark deep-set eyes held hers.

Her heart-shaped face flushed with embarrassment. 'I'm not joking, Sergio. Get rid of her. I don't care how you do it, just *do* it. '

There was hard resolve in his steady appraisal. 'No,' Sergio countered. 'Now calm down.'

Kathy walked away from him. She was trembling with hurt and anger and resentment. She lifted a glass of wine to occupy her restive hands. Her mind and her imagination were on fire with suspicions and fears that there was more going on between Sergio and Grazia than she knew. What was she supposed to think? That everything Grazia had said was true? That Sergio was content for the other woman to attend his wedding because it was part of his revenge? After all, his brother was surely no less guilty of betrayal, but Sergio refused even to speak to Abramo, never mind see him. Grazia, however, was now getting a divorce and, if she was to be believed, that was at Sergio's request. Was that divorce her first step back into Sergio's affections?

Suddenly Kathy was totting up facts and fearing the worst. What was the explanation for Grazia's amazing insider knowledge? How had she known where Kathy would be the night before? Or about Ella's existence? Was Grazia in regular communication with Sergio? Her skin turned clammy. How could Grazia just appear at Kathy's wedding? Why was Sergio protecting the other woman? On this particular very special once-only day, which should have been Kathy's day alone?

All smirking smiles and pearly teeth, Grazia sauntered up to Kathy. 'Trouble in paradise already?' she mocked, making it clear that she had been watching the bride and groom closely.

The next few seconds were for-ever after etched in Kathy's memory. Someone nudged her from behind and tipped her forward. Her arm jerked and, although she contrived to retain her hold on the glass, red wine flew out of it and splashed in a wide arc across Grazia's white dress, leaving stains like drops of blood.

'Oh, my goodness, I'm so sorry!' Kathy gasped, reaching out in haste to snatch up a napkin from the nearest table.

Grazia shrieked as if she had been attacked and refused to let Kathy near her. While the blonde examined the stains with enraged turquoise eyes she hissed at Kathy in vitriolic Italian. Kathy just didn't know what else to do or say but then, mercifully, Maribel surged up out of nowhere like a one-woman rescue squad. Undeterred by Grazia's noisy histrionics, Maribel swept the blonde woman off through the crush and out of sight. A transitory silence as sharp as a thunderclap lay across the ballroom like the quiet before the storm. Then the whispers broke out and grew into a buzz of comment.

A hand closed over Kathy's and drew her round, detaching her fingers from her death grip on the napkin. She looked up at Sergio in bewilderment. Lean, powerful face impassive, he swept her out onto the dance floor in silence.

'It was an accident,' Kathy told him unevenly.

Sergio said nothing. He didn't need to. His dark golden eyes radiated disbelief.

'Say something,' Kathy urged tightly.

'I'm not into arguments as a spectator sport,' Sergio delivered silkily.

Her spine became more rigid. Pain and fury melded inside her until she was literally shaking with the force of her feelings. She pulled back from him with a fixed smile designed to fool any interested onlookers. Engaged in a fierce effort to keep her emotional turmoil hidden, she walked away.

Eyes stinging with tears, Kathy hurried upstairs to the suite she had occupied. Sergio strode through the door only seconds in her wake. 'What the hell did you think you were doing?'

'I didn't throw it at her. Honestly, I've had it with you,' she breathed rawly. 'You won't speak to your brother even though he's a nice guy, but you roll out the red carpet for that spiteful witch at my wedding!'

'When did you meet my brother and reach that conclusion?' Sergio shot at her.

'You're never there when you're needed and you always assume I'm in the wrong,' Kathy told him thickly, ignoring his question. 'Grazia cornered me when I was out last night and bitched at me. She knows too much, she even knows about Ella. This was supposed to be my day and you've wrecked it!'

His ebony brows pleated in surprise. 'Last night? You ran into Grazia in Florence?'

'You wreck everything...every single thing,' Kathy added, mentally piling up his every sin, laying them out for judgement and finding him guilty at that moment without any possibility of forgiveness. 'Now I'm going to pack and I'm returning to London—'

'Kathy—we have just got married,' Sergio pointed out.

'*So?*' Kathy hurled back wrathfully. 'I can already see that I've made a dreadful mistake and I'm not too proud to admit it!'

Sergio rested incredulous golden eyes on her. He lowered lush black lashes, his gaze intent. 'You're not thinking this through—'

'You picked a weak moment to ask me to marry you. I was in labour, for goodness' sake! If I'd been my normal self I'd never have agreed to be your wife. I'm leaving you—'

Sergio moved at speed to plant his lean powerful frame squarely between her and the door. 'No, you're not, *delizia mia.*' He took out his mobile and made a call.

'What are you doing?' Kathy demanded.

'We'll leave together. I may have ruined your day, but that's no reason why we have to share our misery with our hosts and our guests.'

Kathy studied her case, which was already sitting packed in readiness for their departure. She sank down at the foot of the bed. 'You're making me unhappy—'

Sergio moved forward at a measured pace. 'It's early days yet. Obviously, I'm far from perfect. But in my own defence I have to ask why you didn't tell me that you'd met Abramo. Or Grazia?'

'I didn't want to spoil the wedding,' Kathy mumbled in a wobbly voice. 'If you'd wanted me to know about them, you'd have told me about them, right?'

'Please don't cry,' Sergio breathed gruffly, taking a step closer to her. 'Obviously I owe you a little family history…'

His mother had died when he was eight years old. Five years later, his father had married his mistress, Cecilia, who already had a ten-year-old son: Sergio's half-brother, Abramo. Unfortunately, marriage to a man several decades older, who was inclined to frown on her extravagance, failed to meet Cecilia's expectations and she took a series of lovers.

'I minded my own business—' Sergio's lean strong features darkened '—but when my father was receiving cancer treatment, Cecilia began an affair with the family lawyer, Umberto Tessano. He was my father's closest friend and in charge of our business interests.'

Kathy winced. 'What age were you then?'

'Twenty-two, and in my final year at Oxford University. I found my stepmother in bed with Tessano at our London apartment. I felt that I had no choice but to tell my father, but Cecilia and her lover got their story in first.' Sergio vented a bitter laugh of remembrance, his classic profile settling into grim lines.

As the silence dragged Kathy breathed, 'And what was that?'

'That for some time I had been harassing my stepmother with sexual attentions—'

'Oh, no!' Kathy exclaimed with a feeling grimace

'—and that that particular day I made a drunken assault on her virtue from which Tessano gallantly rescued her.'

'Surely your father didn't believe such nonsense?'

'When his lifelong best friend confirmed that sordid account, I had no hope of being believed,' Sergio breathed heavily. 'I had a playboy reputation and Cecilia was beautiful. I can't blame my father because he was a sick man and he loved her. At the time he was dying. I didn't know that but they did. In so far as my father was able within the law, and with Tessano's encouragement, I was disinherited in favour of Cecilia and Abramo. My stepmother married Tessano three months after the funeral.'

His story rocked Kathy out of her self-absorption; she was appalled. There was, she was discovering, a great deal more unpleasantness to the events that had torn Abramo and Sergio apart than she had innocently imagined. The greed and envy of his stepmother and his half-brother had combined to tear Sergio's life asunder. 'Having your father turn against you when he was so ill must've been a nightmare for you.'

'It shattered me.' A muscle pulled taut at the edge of Sergio's wide sensual mouth. 'He died two months later still believing their lies. Up until that point, my life had been easy and privileged. At birth, I was the little prince, the heir to the Azzarini estates and I took it all for granted. Then it was all taken away from me.'

In a quick movement, Kathy got up and reached for his hands in a spontaneous gesture of sympathy, because she had been deeply attached to her own father and she knew how much that misjudgement and rejection from one so close must have tormented Sergio. Her softened green eyes clung to the bold angularity of his bronzed masculine features. 'You should have told me about your family ages ago. But then you don't tell me anything.' Her voice grew more hesitant as she registered that he had finished talking and had still not made a reference to Grazia's role. Feeling self-conscious, she made an abrupt movement to withdraw her hands from his.

'That can change, *dolcezza mia*.' Sergio snapped long brown fingers round her narrow wrists before she could back away again.

Uncertainly, Kathy looked up at him. She was being torn in two by the pull of his white-hot sexual attraction and the need to protect herself from further hurt and disappointment. 'You know you think you're great just the way you are—'

'Until you came along and somehow I consistently manage to live down to your lowest expectations,' Sergio traded.

'Your aversion to weddings…how do you think that made me feel today?' Kathy fenced, jerking her hands free, walking away and turning back with an agitation that betrayed her tension.

'I was a selfish bastard. But, believe me, it wasn't intentional. Grazia jilted me at the altar. It made an indelible impression.'

Shell-shocked by the sheer unexpectedness of that flat admission, Kathy stared up at him.

'Only my closest friends know about that. My father had recently passed away and the wedding was to be a small quiet affair in London. She didn't turn up.' His stunning eyes were dark and reflective. A saturnine smile slashed his hard, handsome mouth. 'Don't look so surprised. Grazia was a luxury I couldn't afford.'

Her lashes veiled her gaze. Her nails carved little crescents into her palms as she recalled Grazia's smiling air of complacency, for the other woman was very much aware of her pulling power. Sergio had wanted her once, loved her enough to want to marry her and lost her again. It could only have added salt to the wound when she decided to marry his brother instead. But it troubled Kathy that both brothers seemed to accept without comment that Grazia put money first.

'Surely she didn't believe that claptrap about you and your stepmother?'

'Naturally not.' Sergio reached out and pulled her up against him with the bold self-assurance that was so much a part of his nature. 'Are you still bent on leaving me?'

Disconcerted by that sudden change of subject, Kathy tipped her coppery head back and he meshed his fingers into the luxuriant fall of her hair to hold her there. Hot golden eyes struck hers and desire pierced her as sharply as a knife. Her tummy flipped and her knees went weak. That fast her physical awareness rose to a level of almost painful sensitivity. His high-voltage male potency got to her every time. She wondered if there had ever been any real chance that she would walk out on him. She wondered if that was a little fantasy she used to console her pride, for at that instant it would have taken brute force to tear her away from him.

'Is it too late to strike a deal?' Sergio husked, tracing the full pout of her lower lip with a caressing fingertip. 'Grant me a trial run until the end of the honeymoon?'

'How flexible are you when it comes to change?' Kathy asked half under her breath. 'Will I need to set objectives? Award points for performance? Come up with rewards for inspirational outcomes?'

'All of the above, *dolcezza mia*.' Brilliant eyes alight with appreciation, Sergio curved her slim body to his. 'Rewards work with me.'

The brisk staccato knock that sounded on the door provoked a groan of frustration from him. 'I said we were leaving immediately.'

CHAPTER NINE

'SO WHAT do you think?' Sergio demanded before Kathy had got more than fifty feet from the helicopter that had delivered them to the Palazzo Azzarini.

Even from the air, the architectural magnificence and size of the building that crowned the hill had disconcerted Kathy. Sergio closed a hand over hers to walk her up the steps to the terrace. 'This house has been in my family for centuries. For the best part of a decade it belonged to Cecilia and Abramo but I bought it back last year. Right now, it's a work of art in progress because the restoration is ongoing. This will be where we base our lives—our home with Ella.'

Kathy cleared her throat gently. 'Objective one, Sergio. Major decisions should be discussed.'

An unholy grin slashed his handsome mouth. 'Of course I'm not going to make you stay here if you hate it. But you're a country girl; you know you are—'

'And when did you reach that conclusion?'

'Maybe I know more about you than you think. You'll love the estate and the people here, *bella mia*.'

Kathy wondered whether to mention that his second objective should be not making assumptions about *her* feelings. But that reference to Ella had tugged at her heart-strings and acted as a distraction. 'I miss Ella already.'

'I'm sure she will be fine without us for a week,' Sergio interposed. 'Maribel is terrific with children.'

Kathy knew that was true. But even though intelligence told her that they needed time alone together as a couple, the habit of constantly fretting about her baby was hard to unlearn and resist. Clearing her mind of those anxious thoughts, she reminded herself of the very sensible pair of nannies also placed in charge of their daughter's care, not to mention the doctor engaged to make daily visits as a safeguard. She rested her hands on the worn stone balustrade, which was still warm from the heat of the day. The silence was bliss after all the hoopla of a big wedding. It was early evening and a soft mist of light lay across the lush valley over which the palazzo presided. Nothing she could see reminded her of the twenty-first century: the rolling hills were covered with dense woodland, vineyards and dotted here and there was the indistinct silvery foliage of olive groves. The view was utterly breathtaking.

She walked below the massive arched portico and wandered wide-eyed into a huge circular reception hall ornamented with faded frescos and towering columns. Like the view, it was an amazing sight and the prospect of living amid such grandeur made her laugh. From somewhere she could hear faint strains of music and she recognised a popular song. Slim hips swaying to the beat, hair glittering like burnished copper and falling back from her high cheekbones, she executed a couple of dance steps.

Sergio fell still and watched her. Kathy met his intent dark eyes and stopped dancing. Although she was pink with embarrassment she gave him an irrepressible grin.

'You have so much life that it bubbles out of you, *bellezza mia*,' he murmured thickly. 'You also look astonishingly beautiful.'

'Who's playing that radio?' she stage whispered.

'Apart from the security outside the house, we should be totally alone here.' Sergio pushed open a door on a big bare room that had scaffolding erected along one wall. A workman's radio was playing in one corner. He switched it off and strolled back to her.

'Thank you. Your first objective at all times,' Kathy instructed cheekily, 'is to make me happy.'

Sergio was much amused. 'And the reward is?'

'Keep me happy and you get an easier life, because you should know by now—I don't suffer in silence.'

Sergio slid out of his jacket and let it fall.

'Oops,' Kathy gasped. 'I think this is a very male take on what makes a woman happy.'

Sergio tugged loose his tie and backed her in the direction of the splendid stone staircase.

'Although you could be on the right track,' Kathy conceded half under her breath, her attention locked to him as he unbuttoned his shirt. 'Of course we could play chess first…'

Sergio was thrown enough by that possibility to frown.

Kathy smiled like the cat that had got the cream. 'Just checking how keen you were. If you'd agreed, I wouldn't have been impressed.'

'*Maremma maiale*…I couldn't concentrate,' he confided.

Her attention rested on the muscular slice of bronzed, hair-roughened torso visible between the parted edges of his shirt. She did not believe that she could have concentrated, either. A delicious frisson of anticipation was already running through her slender body and self-consciousness claimed her, for she wasn't yet used to feeling like that.

Sergio was infinitely more at ease with the ambience. With infinite cool and casualness, he laced his fingers with hers and walked her up the stairs. 'I am not really familiar with shy women—'

'I've never been shy in my life!' Kathy objected, kicking off her shoes there and then on the landing as if she was making a statement.

'Except with me.' Unimpressed by her claim, Sergio lowered his arrogant dark head and let his expert mouth travel a sensual path from her ear lobe to the extended length of her neck and the tiny pulse beating like mad at the centre of her delicate collar-bone. 'And it's okay. I find it unbelievably sexy, *delizia mia*.'

The master bedroom suite was set behind huge double doors and on the same massive scale as everything in the palazzo. Kathy took one look at the gilded four-poster bed and scrambled onto it, bouncing back against the heaped pillows with an ecstatic whoop of appreciation. 'Oh, that's amazing—I've always wanted a bed like this!'

'And although I almost didn't recognise it until it was too late, I always wanted a girl like you in it,' Sergio informed her huskily.

Her ready smile lurched a little and she was quick to lower her lashes to conceal her expression, as she knew that someone like her could not aspire to dream-girl status. She was so different from Grazia in looks, style and experience. As Grazia had cruelly pointed out, she would always be the girl he had idolised as a teenager. There was a history there, a pull of familiarity, background and youthful attachment that Kathy knew she could never hope to equal.

Sergio sank down beside her and undid the clasp of her emerald and pearl necklace, setting it aside before embarking on the tiny hooks on her fitted bodice. Her narrow spine tensed because she was thinking about the moment when he would see the scar on her back. 'That's okay…I can manage!' she said hurriedly, wriggling out of reach with the dexterity of an eel.

Sergio tugged her back to him. 'How did it happen?'

The level of his insight unnerved her and her delicate profile tightened. 'In prison. Someone thought I'd grassed them up and jumped me in the showers.'

He closed his arms round her. 'Nobody will ever harm you again.'

'You can't make promises like that.' Her eyes were hot and scratchy with tears but she wouldn't give way to her emotions. Being absolutely crazy about him was one thing, even dropping a hint of it something else entirely.

Sergio turned her round to look at him. 'You are so terrified of trusting me—'

Her apple-green eyes flashed. 'I'm not terrified of anything!'

Dark golden eyes smouldering, he leant forward and drove her soft lips apart with the passionate demand of his sensual mouth. After so long the taste of him chased through her like a chain reaction. Heat uncoiled in her pelvis while the rest of her turned to jelly. Angling his proud dark head back, he sprang up to peel off his shirt. Her heart thudded while she watched him undress. Light caught the wedding ring on his finger. The reminder that he was her husband was welcome and it strengthened her again.

She slid off the bed in a fluid movement and turned round. 'I need your help to get out of this…' she said gruffly.

He ran down the zip on the fitted skirt and it dropped to her feet. She stepped out of it. He shifted her hair round her slim white shoulders and touched his lips to a sensual pulse point at the vulnerable nape of her neck. 'You're trembling…'

'It's been a long time,' she said breathlessly.

'How long?' His question was abrupt and a sharp little silence fell. 'I did wonder *if*—'

'Don't go there. It's none of your business,' Kathy interposed waspishly. 'Did I ask you for chapter and verse on what you did on your stupid flashy boat?'

'I offered and you refused to listen. Tell me, if I sank *Diva Queen*, would you stop going on about the stag do?' Sergio enquired dulcetly.

Kathy giggled. 'No, I'd tell you how extravagant and wasteful you were, and I still wouldn't forget.'

He let the boned bodice fall and an almost inaudible gasp escaped her when she realised that the jagged seam of her scar was visible. 'You have skin like satin, all soft and silky and white as snow,' he murmured with silken intimacy. 'Your hair looks like flame against it and I can't believe you're so anxious about one small imperfection…' He smoothed over the roughened skin and she shivered, narrow shoulder blades protruding defensively.

'It's ugly,' she pointed out. 'And my skin is so pale it really shows.'

'The only ugliness is in the person who did this to you,' Sergio asserted. 'If it bothers you so much that you feel you have to hide it, a good plastic surgeon could probably make it vanish. But as far as I'm concerned, it's nothing, *bella mia*.'

'You're quite good at saying the right thing when you have to,' Kathy teased, all her tension evaporating, her spine curving as she leant back against him. 'So, no doubt if you put your mind to it, you can be equally good at being married.'

'Is that an order or a request?'

Kathy winced. 'A hint?'

Sergio laughed with rich appreciation and curved possessive hands to her tiny waist. 'It was way too bossy to be a hint.'

His hands closed over the pert swell of her small breasts. She leant back against him with a helpless little moan, shaken by how sensitive she was to that first light touch. The hunger she had fought while Ella needed all her attention was breaking free of her control. A score of times she had watched Sergio walking towards her and she had blocked out the sexual response that had once betrayed her so badly. Those artificial barriers crumpled once she reminded herself that they were married, that, in spite of all the mishaps that had gone before, they were now together. Her soaring sense of relief at that truth made her dizzy.

Filled with sudden impatience, Kathy turned herself round clumsily in the circle of his arms and stretched up on tiptoe to find his mouth for herself. That stolen taste of him was impossibly seductive. He hauled her to him and kissed her with bruising passion, answering the fierce need in her with an accuracy that shook her. He lifted her onto the bed and reached for the silk panties that hugged her hips to peel them off.

Panting for breath, her rosy lips swollen from his attention, Kathy gazed up at him with anxious eyes. Even though she had never felt more naked or exposed, she made no attempt to cover herself up because she accepted that he wanted to look at her. She held her breath in fear that a shadow would cross his face as he suddenly appreciated that she was too skinny and lacking in curves to compete with tiny, curvaceous Grazia, and that her body was marred by the scars of her past and of childbirth.

'You have the most wonderful figure.' Wholly intent on her, Sergio skated an undeniably admiring hand down over her narrow ribcage to a slender thigh still clad in lace-topped white hold-up stockings. 'Elegant, graceful…'

Kathy stretched so that he could better admire her from all angles and ready amusement curved his handsome mouth even as his gaze marked her every move with very masculine appreciation. He shed his boxer shorts without ceremony. She looked at him in turn, for he was beautifully built. The lean, hard, muscular lines of his powerful bronzed body bore out his reputation for being as super fit as an athlete. Her attention rested on his rampant state of arousal and colour warmed her cheeks.

'This is the first place we make a deal, *delizia mia*,' Sergio murmured, pulling her up against his long, sleek, masculine frame

'A deal?' Her green eyes flew wide.

'While I concentrate on what pleases you outside the bedroom you can concentrate on what pleases me *inside* it.'

Kathy studied him in honest wonderment. 'Are you really that basic?'

Sergio nodded affirmation without hesitation. 'I want to spend the entire week in bed,' he growled. 'I am so hungry for you I almost dragged you off from the church.'

Kathy was blushing like mad. But she really liked the idea of being lusted after; a man making her the focus of his erotic intent was most unlikely to be thinking of another woman at the same time.

'Under the table at the reception…into another room… up against the wall…on the floor,' Sergio enumerated thickly. 'In my fantasies you're insatiable, *delizia mia*.'

'Am I?' Kathy whispered a split second before the hungry onslaught of his mouth silenced her.

Fizzing little signals of response darted through her bloodstream and fired inside her with every wicked probe of his tongue. Her body was hypersensitive and geared up for him. For the first time she was eager to touch him and conduct her own explorations. For the first time she was confident enough to be his lover. She traced the solid wall of his chest with admiring fingertips, traversed the taut flatness of his muscular stomach, and when she hesitated he took over to guide and teach her and she learned that it was astonishingly easy to make him groan.

'Enough,' he growled. 'This is our wedding night. I want to give you pleasure.'

'You're so traditional.' Eyes bright as stars, empowered by newly learned skills that had done wonders for her assurance, Kathy flopped back against the pillows. Breathless, she watched him, her gaze clinging to his lean, strong face. There was a wicked tight knot of longing clenched at the heart of her. All he had to do was mention pleasure and she was boneless with expectation.

'No, I've waited too long to lie here and keep my hands off your beautiful body,' Sergio breathed roughly.

Hot, hungry golden eyes assailed her and her mouth ran dry. He spread her beneath him and smoothed a possessive hand over the swollen pink peaks of her breasts. She shivered. A wicked smile of knowledge slashed his strong, sensual mouth.

'You are so ready for me, *amata mia*,' he told her, dipping his tousled dark head to lock his mouth to the tiny taut, straining buds that betrayed her arousal.

Kathy gasped out loud, her hips squirming into the mattress. With controlled passion and endless skill, he traced his sensual path down over her slender twisting length, deliberately not touching her in the one place where she most yearned to be touched. As if in compensation other areas seemed to become much more sensitive in response while the blood thrummed in her veins and her heart pounded faster and faster. A river of elemental fire was flowing through her, burning and scorching everything within its path.

'Sergio…' She almost wept with impatience.

'No orders, instructions or even hints allowed, *cara mia*,' Sergio warned huskily. 'This is one of those occasions when I really do know what I'm doing.'

And she learned things she didn't know about herself. She learned she liked things she had never dreamt she might like. She also learnt a level of response that was terrifyingly powerful. When she believed she could stand no more she found she had no voice to tell him so. He wrested all control, all reasoned thought from her. The ache of need was overwhelming. She was shaking with desire when he chose the optimum moment to take her enjoyment to its zenith. Easing her under him, he plunged into her tender depths with potent power.

Irresistible sensation seized her in a tempestuous flood. He said her name and she moaned a response, locked to him in wild arousal. In thrall to his sexual energy, her excitement soared to a dizzy high. His desire for her was unquenchable, energising. She was all liquid heat and craving. Caught up in a delirium of spellbinding pleasure, she arched her spine and cried out at the height of release. Melting waves of delight followed and left her rocked to the core of her being over the strength of what she had experienced.

'I think I'm going to like being married,' she whispered blissfully, both arms wrapped round him as she hugged him tight with instinctive affection.

An ocean of love and forgiveness was washing round Kathy's heart. She breathed in the musky perfume of his skin and sighed with contentment. He pushed her hair off her brow and kissed her and studied her with slumberous dark-as-night eyes fringed by spiky black lashes. Just looking at him she felt weak. 'You were right,' she added, feeling that just this once a small compliment might be due. 'You don't need instructions.'

The silence lingered and she wondered what he was thinking about. Grazia? The idea and the name came at her out of nowhere and dropped like a giant rock on her floaty feelings to crush them flat. Wasn't it odd that he hadn't even asked what Grazia had said to her the night before? He was certain to have thought about Grazia after seeing her today, Kathy reasoned uneasily. He was only human, but she didn't want him to be only human, and she definitely didn't want him thinking about his former fiancée and soon-to-be-ex-sister-in-law.

'Were you madly in love with Grazia?' Kathy asked abruptly, and she was so horrified by the nosy question that had simply leapt from her brain to her tongue that she almost cringed in front of him.

Sergio released his hold on her and sat up. 'What do you think?'

On the might-as-well-be-hung-for-a-sheep-as-a-lamb principle, Kathy added with equal abruptness, 'Did you speak to her today?'

His jaw line squaring, Sergio groaned out loud. 'No, I think she was only in the building for about ten minutes.'

Her face burning at what might or might not have been an unkind allusion to the incident with the red wine, Kathy muttered, 'She mentioned that she's divorcing your brother.'

Sergio shot her a sudden shuttered glance. Lean, extravagantly handsome features sombre, he vaulted out of bed. 'I need a shower.'

'And you're the guy who's going to change and share things with me?' Kathy flung, cut to the bone and wishing she could shut up—but quite unable in her sense of humiliation and abandonment to make herself shut up.

'*Madonna diavolo*—not stuff like that!' Sergio countered without hesitation.

The bathroom thudded shut. Lesson one, don't mention Grazia, Kathy reflected unhappily. Even after eight years there was unfinished business there. But grilling him like a silly jealous schoolgirl had scarcely been the subtle route to take. She wished she had kept quiet. She wished she hadn't spoiled that lovely precious moment of closeness with prying questions. And over and over again she kept on seeing that hard, closed look on his face.

Ten minutes later, Sergio emerged, black hair slicked back, a towel wrapped round his lean hips. 'Come here, *amata mia*.'

Kathy dealt him an aggrieved look while simultaneously admiring his incredible physique. 'No, I'm sulking,' she confessed from the depths of the four poster.

'Wouldn't you like to cool off in the pool?'

'I can't swim,' she admitted stonily.

Sergio could not hide his surprise. 'Okay. But you'll be safe with me.'

Kathy wondered if there would be shallow steps at one end on which she could sit, because she was very warm and the prospect of cool water on her overheated body was extremely tempting. She hovered between a desire to make him suffer, hurt pride and acceptance.

'I have champagne on ice waiting downstairs.'

'I'm really not into all that vintage stuff,' she told him huffily. 'You're never going to educate my palate.'

'I also have your favourite Swiss chocolate.'

Sergio had saved the best and most seductive offer for last. Her taste buds salivated. As he had discovered one night at the hospital when she had been too afraid to leave Ella to eat, she simply adored chocolate. Her head flipped over, light green eyes arrowing across the room. 'All right—but there is a ground rule. You are not allowed to touch me.'

'Let's see who surrenders first,' Sergio murmured lazily.

Six weeks later, Sergio guided Kathy into a room at the palazzo. As instructed her eyes were tightly shut. He spun her round to heighten the tension.

'Can I look yet?' Kathy demanded.

'Go ahead.'

Kathy blinked: he had taken her out of bright sunlight and it took a while for her eyes to adjust to the dimness. What she saw sitting on a table in front of her was a dolls' house that appeared to be the identical twin of the one she had owned in her childhood, but that she had believed she would never see again. Disconcerted, she simply stared, unable to fathom the coincidence, for she could not believe that it could actually be hers.

'Say something,' Sergio urged.

'It can't be mine…' But she discovered that she was

wrong. When she put out a hesitant hand and opened the front of the miniature house, she found all the little bits and pieces of furniture lined up in tidy ranks for inspection. She lifted the familiar little plastic doll with one leg and dressed in an overlarge knitted frock that her late adoptive mother had made for it.

'It is yours,' Sergio confirmed.

Her attention expanded to encompass the other things on the table-top. She set down the doll to study the collection of cat ornaments, one or two of which had had tails glued back on after getting broken in house moves. There was a bag of girlish keepsakes from her teen years and a little box of jewellery. Beside that sat a collection of photo albums and she leafed through them, suddenly frantic to reach the most important one and there they were—her adoptive parents' photos intact and even spruced up from the faded pictures she recalled. Tears were running down her face without her even realising it.

'Where did you get all this stuff from?' she prompted chokily.

'Your ex-boyfriend still had them—'

'Gareth?' she exclaimed.

'Although his mother sent him to the dump with your possessions, he managed to hide this stuff in the attic. Hey…' Sergio ran a knuckle lightly down her tear stained cheek. 'I wanted to make you smile, not cry!'

'I'm just overwhelmed!' she sobbed, breaking down altogether. 'You don't know what this stuff m-means to me.'

Sergio eased her up against him and stroked a hand through her hair until she had calmed down again. 'But I do. When my father changed his will and deprived me of most of what was to be my inheritance I lost everything below this roof but my clothes. Cecilia and Umberto liquidated the paintings, sculpture and furniture collected by my ancestors, as well as quite a few personal items that I wasn't able to prove belonged to me.'

'You can hardly compare my cat ornaments to a world-renowned art collection—'

'But it was only when I listened to your story that I appreciated how fortunate I was to be in a position to trace and buy back so much of what I lost.'

'If Gareth still had my things, why didn't he answer the letter I sent him after I got out of prison?'

There was a slight hesitation before he responded to her question. 'His mother probably got to it first.'

Kathy paled and looked away from him, conscious that he was uncomfortable with anything that reminded him of her criminal record. 'Did you actually meet Gareth? When?'

Her question acted as a useful distraction because an unholy grin curved Sergio's mobile mouth. 'Last week when I went to London on business. Gareth's mother slammed doors and ranted at him throughout my visit. He leads a dog's life, but at least he had the courage to admit that he still had your possessions and hand them over.'

Kathy was incredibly touched that he had gone to so much trouble on her behalf. 'I can't tell you what this means to me. It's like getting my roots back. When your family's gone, sentimental things mean a lot.' She drew in a deep breath, her green eyes suddenly filling with determination. 'I honestly believe that you should at least talk to your brother and hear what he has to say—'

'I'm not the sentimental type.' His tone was impatient, for it was not the first time she had tried to open the controversial subject.

'You haven't even asked me what Abramo said when he came to see me in London—'

'I'm not interested.'

'He feels really bad about the past and he wants to make peace with you—'

'He almost bankrupted this estate and he's down on his luck. Of course he wants my forgiveness in terms of financial support.'

His cynicism provoked a reproachful look from Kathy. 'He seemed sincere and unhappy and he didn't look at all well,' she sighed. 'All right, I won't say anything more, especially when you gave me such a great surprise.'

'It was nothing.' Sergio curved lean hands to the feminine swell of her slim hips to tug her closer to him. 'Besides, I like it when you think about other people. You have a tender heart, *bella mia*.'

His keen dark eyes held hers and emotion welled up inside her. Sometimes she loved him so much it hurt. Although he had grown up with many privileges he had gone through tough and testing times, just as she had. He set a high value on loyalty, for, while many of his friends had dropped away after his father changed his will, Rashad and Leonidas had demonstrated their support by standing by Sergio and backing his first business ventures.

She understood the experiences that had given him his granite hard core, single-minded sense of purpose and cynicism. The acquisition of a wealth much greater than his own father had ever known had encouraged Sergio's arrogant, ruthless outlook on life. Yet, when he went out of his way to do something that pleased her, Kathy recognised and appreciated how much he had changed where she was concerned. She could hardly credit that six weeks had passed since their wedding because the time had flown in. But then, life didn't stand still around Sergio for longer than five minutes and it was now time for him to get back to his London office. The following day they were due to return to the UK.

Kathy was reluctant to leave Italy because she had been so happy there. The honeymoon had begun with Sergio giving her swimming lessons while banning her from even sitting on the pool steps when he wasn't in the water. He had taken her rock climbing in the Dolomites, as well, teaching her how to sail a catamaran. When she'd got seasick he had made her work through it and she had ended up having a lot of fun. She suspected that her keen sailor husband was determined to get her on board the *Diva Queen*, to which Kathy had taken a fierce dislike sight unseen. She was willing, however, to acknowledge that in physical terms they were both very active and well matched. He was equally convinced that she would love skiing and had already pencilled a winter break into his schedule for that purpose.

Sergio was also encouraging her to take an interest in the charitable trust he had set up and plans had been made for her to accompany him on a trip to Africa to publicise the work being done there. In all the ways that mattered, Sergio was making space for her in his busy, energetic life and sharing his interests to a degree that she had never dared to hope he would. But he had yet to beat her at chess.

Ella remained the centre of their world, the meeting point that continually drew them together and united them. She was beginning to realise that during the first precarious weeks of their daughter's life she had bonded with Sergio at a level she hadn't grasped at the time. They had so shared much and it had added depth to their relationship. Although they had had a fabulous first few days alone as lovers, Sergio had missed Ella as much as Kathy and they had brought her home to join them early.

That afternoon Kathy cuddled Ella and tucked her into her cot for a nap. With her black hair, ever more green eyes and little button nose, Ella was super cute and sometimes Kathy had to force herself to put her daughter down to sleep. She had yet to forget the occasions when it had not been possible for her to hold her baby close.

An hour later, Kathy was just out of the shower when Bridget phoned her to announce that Renzo had asked her to marry him. 'Oh, my goodness, I'm so happy for you!' Kathy exclaimed, anchoring her towel beneath her arms. 'You did say yes, didn't you?'

'Of course I did. He's a good man,' Bridget said fondly. 'He didn't want me to tell you but I think you should know. He's been checking out all the facts of your conviction and the court case and he's been following up every lead for months now.'

Kathy was astonished. 'But why?'

'He accepts that you're innocent and he wants to help. There's some good news, as well. A couple of silver items stolen from old Mrs Taplow's collection were recently acquired by an antique trader in Dover. He listed them on his website and Renzo spotted them. If he can trace them back to whoever sold them, he might be able to identify the real thief.'

Kathy frowned. 'It's really kind of him to take such an interest, so please tell him how much I appreciate it. But I think too much time has passed. People won't remember anything—'

'Don't be so pessimistic,' Bridget scolded. 'The trader called in the police and it's already being investigated. The guy bought the silver in good faith and he stands to lose a lot of money. Aren't you dying to know who the thief is? Of course you are!'

Kathy grimaced, for she had long since worked out the likely identity of the thief. Only one person had had the opportunity to lay the fake trail that had led to Kathy being convicted of a crime she hadn't committed. But Kathy did not know how she could possibly prove the fact. Rather than burn up in self-destructive bitterness, she had chosen to get on with her life. Four years on, she had little time for false hopes and accepted that she would have to live with a criminal record to the end of her days.

'Let's hope for the best,' Kathy responded with tact. 'So when do you think you'll be getting married?'

'Well, we don't want to wait long.'

'I think it's past time we let Sergio in on the secret—'

'Renzo didn't think it would be *professional* to admit that we were a couple before your wedding,' Bridget shared ruefully. 'Men!'

'What secret?'

Thrown off balance by the interruption, Kathy spun round and saw Sergio poised in the doorway. His lean dark features were grim. 'Kathy…I asked you a question.'

His commanding tone made Kathy redden with annoyance. Wondering what on earth was the matter with him, she made a hurried excuse and promised to call Bridget back later. She set the receiver down and moved forward. 'Bridget and Renzo have been dating for months and he's just asked her to marry him. That was the secret but it wasn't mine to share.'

Sergio regarded her closely, not a muscle moving on his lean strong face, his shrewd dark eyes unrevealing. 'I had no idea that they were seeing each other, but Renzo's private life is not my concern.'

Her tension increased, for she could tell that something was wrong. 'Why are you angry with me?'

'I'm not angry. But I'm afraid there's been a change of plan. We're leaving now, not tomorrow morning.'

Her smooth brow indented. 'Now? Like, *right* now? I'm just out of the shower!'

'I would really appreciate it if you were ready to leave in ten minutes,' Sergio drawled.

'But I haven't even packed!'

'The staff will deal with that. Just get dressed.'

Obviously something had happened. Anxious now, she put on a green dress that he had admired on her a few days earlier and paused only to pin up her damp copper hair with a clip. Sergio was on the terrace talking urgently into his phone. One glance and her husband still took her breath away. Black hair gleaming in the sunlight, his classic profile in evidence, he was the living image of sleek Italian sophistication in a caramel linen jacket worn with the sleeves pushed up and teamed with pale fitted jeans.

Kathy approached him as he switched off the phone. 'Please tell me what's up.'

'Nothing unexpected, *amata mia*.' Stunning dark golden eyes rested on her worried face. He strolled over to her and bent his arrogant dark head to crush her full pink lips beneath his.

The erotic probe of his tongue set off an alert through every nerve-ending in her slender body. At her most vulnerable, she quivered in bewildered response. Her senses singing, she leant into the muscular heat of his tall, powerful frame. Freeing her again, he closed a hand over hers and urged her down the steps to the helipad.

'You never said where we were going,' Kathy said breathlessly.

Sergio helped her into the helicopter. Ella was already snuggled in a safety seat demonstrating her amazing ability to sleep like a log through every interruption and noise. 'No, I didn't, did I?'

The mystery was cleared up within the hour. The pilot flew out over the Mediterranean and just as the light was fading in rosy golden splendour across the sky landed on a vast ocean-going yacht.

Fifteen minutes later, Ella was stashed in another cot in a cabin with her excited nannies in tow. Kathy joined Sergio in the dazzlingly plush décor of the main reception area. 'So what's going on?' she pressed, fed up with being kept in the dark…

'Leonidas has a lot of media connections. He warned me that tomorrow a tabloid newspaper is running a story on your criminal record,' Sergio explained, his strong jaw line clenching. 'I decided it would be a good idea to keep you and Ella somewhere the cameras can't get near you. While *Diva Queen* stays out at sea, you're safe.'

Shock hit Kathy in a wave of physical reactions. The colour drained from her complexion and nausea upset her tummy. Feeling sick and dizzy, she sank down on the nearest seat in silence. A split second after that, other responses kicked in and they hurt her a great deal more, for she discovered that she no longer had the courage to meet her husband's gaze for fear of what she might see there. Revulsion, anger, derision? How could she blame him for loathing the public exposure of her shameful, embarrassing past? What decent man wanted it known that his wife had once been prosecuted for stealing from a sick old lady?

Yet there was nothing, absolutely nothing, Kathy acknowledged wretchedly, that she could do to change the situation.

CHAPTER TEN

'I'M SORRY about this,' Kathy admitted tightly.

'I believe we were both aware that this situation was on the cards,' Sergio countered levelly. 'But I'm surprised it's happened so quickly.'

Kathy had still to look at him. Coffee was served. Her heart was thumping in what felt like the foot of her throat and the sick hollowness in her tummy was refusing to abate. Oh, yes, she was sorry all right. Even though she had served her time in prison her conviction was still the equivalent of a giant rock anchored to her ankle. And it seemed that it always would be.

But what was really tearing her apart was the change in Sergio. He was not a male who could ever have envisaged having a wife who was a social embarrassment. She could not forget that he had once tried to persuade her to change her name and move to France to escape her past. Now his forecast of public humiliation was coming true and it was a miracle that her Alpha male had yet to voice a single I-told-you-so. A total miracle, Kathy conceded miserably. His cool façade of formality could only be concealing the furious frustration that he felt he had to contain.

'Fortunately, I did prepare for this eventuality,' Sergio informed her.

'Am I going to disappear at sea?' Kathy mumbled, for in her opinion only a bigger scandal would wipe out the one about to break.

The silence was electrifying.

Sergio released his breath in a slow hiss. 'That's not funny, Kathy.'

Kathy had rarely felt less like laughing. There was an intolerable ache of tears in her throat. Only hours earlier, she had been naively rejoicing in her contentment. In so far as he was able, Sergio had contrived to forget her prison record. But it would be foolish to ignore the fact that Sergio had conservative views on crime and punishment. He abhorred dishonesty. He was ashamed of her now. How could he not be? He was striving to be sympathetic, but she could sense his reserve like a wall inside him.

How had he felt when Leonidas Pallis had warned him of the story about to break? The cringe factor during that conversation must have been high, she thought guiltily. Leonidas might be one of his oldest friends, but men didn't like showing a more vulnerable side to each other and a wife who was a former jailbird could only be a source of severe embarrassment. How much shame could any marriage stand? How could he continue to respect her? For how long would Sergio overlook her past without thinking of her as a liability he could do without? He was very proud of the Torrente name and here she was dragging it through the mire. He had wanted her past to stay hidden to protect their child. All of a sudden she was seeing how events could conspire to destroy their relationship.

Kathy made a courageous effort to pull herself together. 'You were saying,' she muttered in a wobbly undertone, 'that you had prepared for this?'

'*Maremma maiale,*' Sergio groaned, crossing the room to propel her up out of her seat and into the protective circle of his arms. 'We'll get through this, *bella mia*. It's a matter of damage limitation.'

Held close and comforted, Kathy gulped back the tears threatening and nodded vigorously into a broad masculine shoulder. He felt strong and familiar and she wanted to stay in his arms for ever.

'My PR team have come up with a press statement that strikes the right note,' Sergio declared, settling her down onto a sofa. 'It will end the speculation. Next week someone else will be the target.'

Kathy wasn't quite sure she understood what he was saying, but his concern for her had banished her fear of losing him and strengthened her. 'All right.'

His spectacular dark gaze was intent. 'It's not what you have done, but how you handle it once it's in the public arena that matters.'

Kathy gave him an uncertain nod. 'This statement…'

'I have a copy of it here.' Sergio extracted a sheet of paper from a file and extended it for her perusal. 'It's standard stuff and with your agreement, it will be released to the press.'

Kathy had only read the first sentence when her heart started to sink. It was basically an acknowledgement of her conviction for theft, a reference to the fact that she had served the sentence for her wrongdoing and the assurance that she had learned her lesson. An everyday tale of retribution and redemption.

'I can't allow you to release this to the media,' she whispered tautly.

'Public apology—that's what it takes now. It may seem

glib and pointless, but people will respect you for being honest about your past.'

'Sergio…' There was a desperate plea for understanding in Kathy's troubled gaze. 'I am not a thief. I didn't take that silver. I went to prison for something I didn't do. I can't agree to this statement being made on my behalf because it would be a lie.'

'That press release will draw a line under the whole affair and take the steam out of the story.'

'Did you even listen to what I just said?'

'You already know where I stand on that issue,' Sergio breathed in a driven undertone. 'Maybe you need to forgive yourself for what you did before you can come to terms with it. But right at this moment we have something more immediate to deal with—'

Her cheekbones flushed with annoyance, Kathy flew to her feet. 'I can't believe you just said that to me!'

An expression of hard resolve was stamped on Sergio's lean, darkly handsome features. 'You made a mistake when you were young and you had no family to support you. Many teenagers have made similar mistakes, put them behind them and gone on to live law-abiding lives just as you have done. You should be proud of that achievement.'

'Stuff the pep talk! There's only one little problem—I didn't make that mistake in the first place!' Kathy fired back at him. 'You've never even let me tell you what happened.'

'You avoid the subject like the plague.'

Kathy froze in surprise. She was dismayed that her desire to stay away from a controversial issue during their honeymoon had given him that misleading impression. And a heartbeat later she was furious with herself for being so craven.

'Don't treat me like your enemy. I'm trying to help you,' Sergio spelt out grimly.

Kathy compressed bloodless lips. 'I know.'

'Will you agree to the statement?' Sergio demanded.

Kathy turned as pale as a martyr at the stake. 'No, never.'

Sergio dealt her a forbidding appraisal. 'This problem will run and run. It won't go away. It has to be dealt with.'

The expectant silence that stretched was like an icy hand trailing down her taut spine, but she defied that intimidation. Her apple-green eyes alight with resolve, she tilted her chin. 'But not like this. Not with me making a fake confession and a fake apology for something I didn't do. I served my full sentence because I wouldn't lie and express remorse for someone else's crime.'

Sergio surveyed her with cold, hard censure in his challenging gaze. The trauma of that moment made her stop breathing. Without another word, he turned on his heel and strode out of the room. Pulling in a jagged breath, she collapsed down on a seat and stared into space. *What if this costs me my marriage? What if I lose him?* Her mind was awash and adrift on terrified thoughts and fears.

It didn't help that she could see his point. He had decided she was guilty at a very early stage of their relationship when he hardly knew her, and he was as stubborn as a mule. He had even got as far as explaining her criminal behaviour to his own satisfaction—youthful mistake, no family backup. In trying circumstances, he had not voiced a single word of blame or complaint. And now he was engaging in what he had called damage limitation in an effort to protect what little remained of her reputation. Determined to keep her safe from the paparazzi, he had marooned her on his yacht. He was doing what came most naturally to him: taking charge, making decisive moves to handle the crisis and trying to protect her, as well. But instead of being grateful for his advice, she was being unreasonable and refusing it. She dashed the tears from her eyes with a trembling hand.

An evening meal was served in the dining room. Although the table was set for two and she waited and the steward hovered in readiness, Sergio didn't appear. She ate hardly anything and at her request was shown to a huge stateroom. Desperate to fill the time, she ran a bath in the amazing splendour of the marble bathroom. She had only lowered herself into the warm scented water when the door she had forgotten to shut opened wider to disclose Sergio.

A dark shadow of stubble roughening his hard jaw line, black hair tousled, his shirt hanging loose from his jeans, he had so much raw bad-boy appeal he made her heart bounce like a ball inside her chest. As she sat up in haste, hugging her knees to her breasts, he regarded her in nerve-racking silence.

'I'm sorry…' he said grittily.

Those two words were like the blade of a knife slicing between her ribs, as she didn't know what was coming next. Even worse where he was concerned, she was in negative mode and expecting bad news. What was he sorry for? An inability to live with a woman publicly branded a thief?

Sergio shrugged a broad shoulder. His gorgeous tawny eyes were strained. 'I don't know what to say to you.'

Kathy was frozen there in the bath like an ice statue, the gooseflesh of fear breaking out on her skin and a clammy sensation in her tummy.

'You see it was your fatal flaw,' he added incomprehensibly.

'What was?'

'I've always had this theory that everyone has a fatal flaw. Yours was a criminal record,' he shared. 'It all connected, it made sense—'

'What made sense?' Kathy was hanging on his every word and wishing they would connect in an understandable way.

'You were beautiful, clever and sexy, but you were working in a menial position for low pay. Why? You had a criminal record.' Sergio flattened his strong, sensual mouth. 'I'm a cynic. I always look on the dark side. It never occurred to me to doubt that you were a thief.'

'I know,' she agreed heavily.

'And for months I didn't think about it because when I thought about it I got annoyed,' he breathed almost roughly. 'When I found you again and Ella was born, I let that knowledge go—I buried it.'

Her green eyes only accentuated her pallor. Her supposed guilt had been buried like a body because that was the only way he could live with it and her.

Sergio shifted an eloquent brown hand to signify his regret and then said something that disconcerted her entirely. 'But although a jury found you guilty and you went to prison you are not a thief.'

Her smooth brow indented. 'What did you just say?'

'I believe you. You've convinced me, *dolcezza mia*.'

Kathy continued to stare at him in wordless disorientation, for that change of heart and opinion knocked her sideways.

'You're innocent. You've got to be. It doesn't make sense any other way. I'm sorry I wouldn't listen.'

'I don't understand why you're willing to listen now,' she admitted unevenly.

'I weighed up the crime with everything I know about

you and all of a sudden it was clear to me that you had to be telling me the truth.'

'Have you been talking to Renzo, by any chance?'

'No. Why?'

Sergio had no idea that his security chief had been looking into her case, acquainting himself with the facts and chasing up every possible lead. When Kathy explained, his lean powerful face shadowed. 'So, even Renzo believed you when I didn't.'

'I imagine Bridget wouldn't have given him any choice in the matter.' The relief of knowing that Sergio finally had faith in her brought a tidal wave of tears to the back of her eyes. She studied the water fixedly and blinked like mad. 'Let me finish my bath. I'll be out in five minutes.'

Sergio frowned. 'Are you going to cry?'

Kathy raised a delicate brow, her eyes bright as jewels. 'What do you think?'

'I need to know what happened to you four years ago. Your arrest, the whole story.'

'It's not likely to make you feel any better.'

'Do you think I deserve to feel better?'

'No,' she said honestly.

Kathy didn't cry. He had given her good news. At last he believed that she wasn't a thief. It had only taken him the guts of a year to reach that happy conclusion but, hey, later was better than never. She put on a crisp blue cotton robe and went into the bedroom to join him.

'I was hired to act as Mrs Taplow's companion and provide her with basic meals by her nieces, Janet and Sylvia. I hardly ever saw Sylvia because she worked. They lived in the village about a mile away,' Kathy told him, curling up on the giant bed. 'Mrs Taplow lived in a big old house. On my first day Janet explained that her aunt was suffering from the early stages of dementia and that I should pay no heed to her stories about her things disappearing.'

Sergio elevated an ebony brow and sat down on the bed beside her. 'Didn't that make you suspicious?'

'No. I was too glad of the job and somewhere to live. The old lady did seem a little confused sometimes but she was very nice,' Kathy confided ruefully. 'Janet asked me to clean the silver, which was kept in a cupboard, and she told me that it was very old and valuable. There was a lot of it and, to be honest, I barely looked at the stuff as I cleaned it.'

'But no doubt you put your fingerprints all over it.'

'A few weeks later Mrs Taplow got very upset and claimed that two pieces of silver had gone missing. I couldn't have said either way, but I mentioned it to Janet and she said her aunt was either imagining things or that she had removed them herself and hidden them somewhere. She insisted that Mrs Taplow had done that before. Mrs Taplow wanted to call the police, but I dissuaded her,' Kathy recalled unhappily.

Sergio closed a reassuring hand over hers. 'What happened next?'

'The same thing again—but I noticed the pieces that had gone missing and I searched all over the house for them without any luck. I started feeling uncomfortable, but Janet told me not to be silly and that the items would turn up eventually. I had no reason to doubt her. I had a day off. I was supposed to be meeting Gareth and I was getting dressed when the police arrived,' Kathy whispered, sick at the memory of the moment when her world had begun to come crashing down around her. 'They searched my room and the

Georgian jug was found in my handbag. I was charged with theft. I thought maybe the old lady had put it in there, but then I was told that she didn't suffer from dementia.'

'*Madonna diavolo*…you were hired and set up, so that her niece could steal from her and ensure that you got the blame.' His dark eyes were grim.

'But there was no way of proving it when Janet denied it. It was my word against hers and she was a church warden. There was a large amount of money involved in the silver that had gone missing.'

'But the evidence was circumstantial.'

'Three different solicitors dealt with my case, but I was still convinced that I'd be proved innocent. I didn't really understand how much trouble I was in,' Kathy admitted shakily. 'I was in shock for days after the guilty verdict and it was too late then. There was nobody on the outside to fight my corner.'

Sergio tried to retain a hold on her hand but she trailed her fingers free and turned her head away. He sprang upright and moved back into her field of vision. 'It must have been a terrifying ordeal.'

Kathy lifted a narrow shoulder in a jerky shrug.

Tall, dark and impossibly handsome, Sergio hovered at the foot of the bed. 'I had no idea, *amata mia*. I feel like a total bastard.'

'Don't. Let it go. I don't blame you for thinking the worst. Plenty of other people have reacted the same way,' she told him ruefully. 'But it consumed too many years of my life and I don't want to waste any more time on regret.'

'However long it takes I will clear your name. I swear it,' Sergio intoned in a raw undertone.

'Is it that important to you?'

Sergio dealt her a questioning look. 'Of course it is. You're my wife.'

It was the early hours before Sergio came to bed that night and she noticed that he didn't reach for her the way he usually did. In fact, it was the very first night they had ever spent together when they slept so far apart that they might as well have been in separate beds. The next morning he was gone when she awakened and she thought unhappily that that might be for the best.

While Kathy had no desire to read what the newspapers made of her criminal conviction, she had the sinking suspicion that Sergio would read every word and feel the humiliating sting of it to the primal depths of his macho soul. As a result she had no appetite for breakfast and she passed most of the day with Ella, worrying about the future of their marriage. After all, while he might accept that she had been wrongfully convicted, he still had to live in a world where everybody else would most assuredly believe his wife was guilty as charged. He wasn't in love with her, so there was no safety net to strengthen them when things went wrong; there was no reservoir of forgiving love and tolerance to draw on.

Late afternoon, Sergio strode in, dressed in a black business suit teamed with a gold tie. He looked extraordinarily handsome and unusually tense and pale. Black lashed dark eyes inspected her. 'I've been flat out all day but you usually walk in and out of my office when I'm working, *bella mia*. Where were you?'

In the strained atmosphere, Kathy veiled her troubled gaze. She had lost the confidence to assume that she would be welcome. In addition, his personal staff had flown in early that morning and would presumably have read all about their employer's jailbird wife. On a day when she really just wanted to hide herself away a brave smile of indifference had proved too much of a challenge. She had also feared that her presence would embarrass him. 'With Ella…I forgot you were going to London tonight.'

'Twenty-four hours max and I'll be back. I don't like leaving you.'

'I'm fine,' Kathy hastened to protest, for a woman who needed looking after like a child could hardly be an attractive prospect to a male as independent as he was.

'By the way, that newspaper article? It was nothing.' Sergio shrugged but failed to meet her gaze. 'Don't worry about it.'

But she did; she couldn't help it. Guilty or otherwise, she had become a source of embarrassment. His reserved manner warned her that events had hit him hard. Both Tilda and Maribel rang her that evening and proved their worth as loyal friends. Tilda invited her and Sergio to spend a weekend in Bakhar and Maribel offered to stay on the yacht with Kathy for a few days. Kathy thanked her and gently refused. The next day, Sergio phoned and told her that he would be away longer than he had expected.

Forty-eight hours after that, Kathy flicked on the television in the bedroom and up came the Italian news channel that Sergio always watched. Before she could change station, her husband's picture appeared on screen and her hand stilled on the remote control. That was swiftly followed by film of Grazia emerging from a hotel and Sergio emerging from what looked like the same building. Her grasp of Italian wasn't good enough to translate the accompanying commentary. She had to use the internet to check the report out and, although there was very little information available, what she found out shattered her.

The night before, Sergio had spent a couple of hours in the same London hotel as Grazia, both of them leaving by separate entrances in an evident effort to avoid detection. There was talk of a reanimated affair with reference made to Grazia's divorce and Sergio's marriage described as being 'in turmoil' after unsavoury revelations about his wife's past.

The phone rang.

The instant Kathy heard Sergio's deep pitched drawl she interrupted, 'What were you doing in a hotel with Grazia?'

'Malicious gossip travels faster than an avalanche,' he murmured smooth as glass. 'I'll be with you in an hour.'

'You didn't answer my question.'

'I have company, *cara mia*.'

At her end of the phone, she reddened fierily in receipt of that clarification. Time had never seemed to move more slowly than in the minutes that followed. She left the bedroom and waited in the entertainment-sized lounge, where she paced the floor. Eventually she walked out onto the deck where the blue sky was beginning to shade with warm hints of peach as the sun began to go down.

She could not imagine life without Sergio, but she was wondering if, at the end of the day, that might also be how Sergio felt about Grazia. A fatal attraction that he despised, but ultimately couldn't resist. Would that explain why was he was so reluctant to talk about his former fiancée? He had still to ask what Grazia had said to his bride the night before their wedding. Kathy could only feel threatened by that reality.

Her heart started beating very fast when the helicopter came in low to land. Lean, powerful face serious, Sergio emerged.

'For once, I have good news,' he informed her levelly. 'Janet Taplow was arrested this afternoon.'

That being the last topic she had expected him to open the conversation with, Kathy simply stared back at him. 'Are you serious?'

'The police got a search warrant and found the old lady's missing silver in her house. Mrs Taplow died last year. Janet only began selling off the silver a few months ago when she thought it would be safe to do so. But as you're already aware, Renzo was able to identify a piece of it and the trail led straight back to her.'

'My word...' Her legs hollow with shock, Kathy weakly sat down on the arm of a designer sofa. 'After all this time, the truth is coming out—'

'An antique dealer has made a positive identification of Janet, and her cousin is also willing to give evidence against her because she's furious at being robbed of a large part of what should have been a shared inheritance. I've got my best lawyers working on this. It'll take time but they are certain that you will eventually be able to prove your innocence.'

Kathy pressed cooling hands to her shaken face. 'I can't believe it. I don't know how to thank you—'

'This is all thanks to Renzo's efforts. He's the hero here. But for your intervention, he would no longer be on my staff. I've done nothing,' Sergio declared. 'The tabloids are already onto this development. A wrongful conviction is more newsworthy than the original story. You'll probably be inundated with requests for interviews about your experiences in prison.'

Kathy pulled a face at the idea. 'No, thanks.'

'How do you feel?'

'Shocked.' Kathy hesitated. 'What about Grazia?'

Sergio raked long fingers through his cropped black hair. 'I had no choice but to do a deal with her face to face. But I should've guessed she would have the paparazzi standing by to capture those photos at the hotel. Grazia never misses out on free publicity.'

Kathy frowned. 'What sort of a deal?'

'Abramo was in London because he's been receiving treatment for leukaemia. He's not well at all,' Sergio told her heavily.

'Oh, my goodness, you finally got in touch with your brother!' Her lovely face sobered as she registered what he had said. 'Leukaemia?'

Sergio grimaced. 'His chances are roughly fifty-fifty. He doesn't need the stress of a contested divorce right now, so I bought her off.'

'That's what you mean by a deal? You gave Grazia money?'

'In return for certain undertakings all legally signed, sealed and delivered.' Sergio withdrew a document from his jacket and unfolded it. 'Our hotel rendezvous was supported by a team of lawyers. They did well. I would have paid twice as much.'

Kathy was nodding like a puppet in rapid succession. 'What undertakings?'

'Grazia has agreed to return the family jewels in her possession and give Abramo a quiet divorce. She has also promised not to approach you again.'

Her green eyes widened in surprise. 'You mean you were annoyed when she cornered me at that club?'

'Of course!'

'Well, why didn't you say so then?'

Sergio regarded her with bleak dark-as-night eyes. A faint veil of colour accentuated his hard cheekbones. 'I felt very guilty about what happened and guilt made me lash out. She upset you before our wedding and almost ruined the day—'

'How did she even find me that night?'

'The nightclub manager tipped her off.'

'She knew about Ella.'

'But not from me,' Sergio countered, letting her know that he understood her concerns.

'Grazia said you told her to divorce Abramo.'

'No, that was a lie. But it was my fault that she made you the target of her venom,' Sergio said gravely.

'How could it be your fault?'

'Grazia's a vulture. When she tried to get back into my life, I didn't discourage her as much as I could have done and her vanity was her undoing,' Sergio revealed with visible reluctance. 'Her pursuit amused me. It was before I met you and I didn't see why I shouldn't play her along as she had once done to me—'

'You wanted revenge?' Kathy was startled by a possibility that she had not considered before, and uplifted by the belated awareness that he was no longer interested in the beautiful blonde.

Sergio shifted a dismissive brown hand. 'I would never have sought her out on my own behalf; I didn't care enough. But I was angry when she dared to approach me last year. I didn't have to do anything to settle old scores— just stand back and watch while Grazia plotted and planned to get me back.'

Kathy released a shaken sound of consternation. 'But she was Abramo's wife.'

'Grazia goes where the money is and the minute Abramo lost his, he was yesterday's news. He knows that as well as I do and I do believe he is over her now. What kind of a woman deserts her husband when he's ill?'

'A ruthless one—the sort of woman I thought you admired.'

'But she'd never beat me at chess in a million years, *delizia mia*. She'd never dream of telling me I can't climb Everest because it's too dangerous and I might get killed—by the way, I did it a few years ago. I think it's fortunate that I took in certain experiences before I met you because there's a long list of manly sporting pursuits which bring you out in a rash of anxiety, isn't there?'

Kathy had turned pink with mortification, not having appreciated that her terror at the prospect of anything happening to him was quite so obvious.

Sergio rested dark golden eyes on her and reached for her hands. 'Grazia would have encouraged me to follow dangerous sports because she'd have enjoyed being a merry widow more than wife. How could you think I'd want her back for even five minutes when you were around?'

'You and I sort of fell into a relationship. Nothing was planned—especially not Ella.' Kathy's voice was uneven. 'But you chose Grazia. You wanted to marry her.'

'*Per meraviglia,*' Sergio sighed in a tone of regret. 'I was twenty-one and she was a trophy my friends envied. I loved her to the best of my ability then. I was a boy, but now I'm a man and I have a very different take on what I want in a wife. But until I met you I didn't know what I wanted—'

'All you wanted was sex,' Kathy told him bluntly.

'That may be how I first saw us, but you taught me to want other things that I didn't even know that I needed.'

'Like what?' she prompted.

'Ordinary things like laughter, honest opinions, arguments…'

'You think you needed someone to argue with?'

'Opposition is good for me now and again. And the occasional intelligent dialogue that did not relate to jewellery, clothes or diet was very welcome, *amata mia*,' Sergio confided. 'Of course, I didn't properly appreciate what a catch you were until you vanished for seven and a half months and I found out what it was like to miss you.'

Kathy was enthralled, for at first she had thought he was teasing her but now she was recognising the sincerity that lay behind the self-mocking delivery. 'You missed me?'

'And it was too late. You were gone. Now if Grazia had played that card she would've shown up again within a couple of weeks, but, you being you, you were gone for good.'

'I thought it was for the best at the time.'

'The knowledge that I came that close to losing you for ever still haunts me. The stag cruise was a disaster. No…' Sergio groaned when she suddenly snatched her hands from his. 'You have to let me talk about this—'

Her face tight, Kathy stepped back from him. 'No, that kind of stuff is better left buried. It was before we were married and none of my business.'

Sergio strode forward and swept her up off her feet. 'Oh, I like that when it's still being held against me and thrown up at every opportunity!'

'When did I last throw it up?' Kathy yelled.

'You didn't see the judgemental look on your face when you got on this boat for the first time…'

'Maybe your conscience made you imagine that. For goodness' sake, put me down!'

'No. I didn't get horrendously drunk on that stag cruise. I didn't even kiss anyone. Okay?' he demanded. 'You were inside my head to such an extent you might as well have been with me. You were the only woman I wanted.'

Shocked by that burst of confession, Kathy let him carry her downstairs to their stateroom. 'I didn't like you very much then.'

Sergio laid her down very gently on the bed. His brilliant dark eyes were bleak. 'I know and it's what I deserved, totally what I asked for. But I'll never be like that with you again because I love you. Even if you were a thief I would still be married to you and I would still feel the same way.'

Kathy was stunned by the raw emotion stamped in his face. 'You fell for me?'

'Probably the first time we met and my brain started malfunctioning. I was all over the place, assuming this, assuming that about you. The sex was amazing, but so were you. When I was in Norway, the rest of the guys were in stitches at the number of times I phoned you.'

'Yes, you did phone quite a bit,' she acknowledged.

'And the move to France may not have appealed to you, but it was my first fumbling attempt at a committed relationship in a decade,' Sergio argued in his own defence.

'I'm glad you used the word *fumbling*.'

'And I blew any remaining goodwill with that stupid stag do. I accept that. But when I couldn't find you, I was devastated. That's when I knew how I felt about you. That's why there was nobody else all that time…'

'Nobody?' Wide-eyed, Kathy turned her coppery head to study him. 'Not one single woman in all those months?'

'Call it retribution for the night I made you sleep with me. I haven't been with anyone else since I met you and

I'm amazingly proud of that fact.' His rueful smile tilted her heart on its axis. 'I did get you to agree to marry me in a weak moment. It was deliberate. I knew I wouldn't feel secure until you were my wife. I would have done virtually anything to get that ring on your finger.'

Kathy was smiling back, flattered by such eagerness to marry on his part. 'So it was really just the wedding hoopla you disliked? Not the act of getting married to me?'

'Is that what you thought?' Sergio grimaced. 'It wasn't meant that way, *bella mia*. I thought I could make you happy—'

'You did.'

'But all the time I was making the worst mistake I could in not believing in you. I feel very guilty about that.'

'It's true you've got flaws, but I love you anyway—or maybe even because of them. I don't think I could stand you if you never did anything wrong but don't take that as an invitation to stray.' A luminous smile curved her rosy mouth while he studied her in wonderment. 'Because as you know—the stag thingy—I'm not forgiving about stuff like that—'

On his knees on the bed, he hauled her to him and kissed her with a passionate intensity that made her blink back tears of happiness.

'And what is more, a good husband keeps his energy for his wife,' Kathy told him dizzily, yanking off his tie.

Sergio pitched off his jacket and wrenched at his shirt with considerable enthusiasm. 'How the hell did you manage to fall in love with me?'

'You're annoying, but very good-looking, sexy, entertaining…' Kathy spread admiring fingertips on his bronzed and muscular chest, but her eyes were soft and bright and loving. 'I have to confess that when I beat you at chess it gives me a thrill—'

In answer Sergio tipped her back against the soft pillows and kissed her breathless. His rampant enthusiasm met with a most encouraging reception.

Almost three years later, Kathy put the finishing touches to her make-up, smoothed her vibrant copper hair into place and stood back to get the full effect of her shimmering golden ball gown.

Within the hour, everybody who was anybody would be arriving at the Palazzo Azzarini, because Sergio Torrente was throwing what was being described as the party of the year. Why? A miscarriage of justice had been declared in Kathy's case and her wrongful conviction as a thief quashed. The judge during the original court case was also deemed to have misdirected the jury, thus preventing her from receiving a fair hearing. She had had the support of a wonderful legal team, who had had to work long and hard to achieve that successful result even though Janet Taplow had finally owned up to planting the jug in Kathy's bag.

Indeed Janet Taplow had ironically already served her sentence and won her release by the time Kathy contrived to clear her own name. But Kathy had not been bothered by that reality. It was enough for her that the truth be known. When she received compensation for her imprisonment she planned to donate it to a charity that helped former offenders to settle back into the community and find work.

No longer haunted by painful bitter memories, she was at last managing to leave the past behind her. Little by little, she was regaining the easy confidence and friendliness that had once been so much a part of her personality. Her happiness had contributed most to that process.

Bridget and Renzo had recently celebrated their second wedding anniversary. Bridget was now the mother of a little boy of six months, a development that had surprised and delighted the older woman, who had assumed she was at an age when a pregnancy was an unlikely event. Abramo had recovered from his illness and started dating again. Sergio was slowly forging stronger bonds with his half-brother and had put him in charge of one of his smaller companies. Grazia had collected a small fortune off Sergio and had gone on to become the fourth wife of a fabulously wealthy Egyptian. Like Cleopatra, she was said to bathe in milk and honey.

Kathy had spent most of the first two years of her marriage based in London so that she could take classes and complete the business degree she had been working on when she had first met Sergio. Maribel Pallis had become one of her closest friends. Sergio and Kathy also regularly visited Bakhar to enjoy Rashad and Tilda's lavish hospitality with Maribel and Leonidas. Their children all knew each other very well.

Kathy put on her jewellery, a recent birthday present from Sergio. The contemporary diamond pendant glittered with white-fire brilliance at her throat and the earrings caught the light with every movement. She went to say goodnight to Ella, with her pet Siamese cat, Horace, padding fluidly in her wake. Already Horace was like her shadow and he had almost—but not quite—filled the space left by his much-missed predecessor, Tigger.

Ella was still awake and complaining about Elias Pallis, who was almost three years older. In truth, Elias and Ella frequently fought like cat and dog. Elias liked to lay down the law and Ella couldn't stand being told what to do. Tilda's son, Sharaf, was always the peacemaker, very much a future diplomatist and ruler in the making while Bethany, his little sister, was as feisty as Ella. Soon, Kathy reflected dreamily, resting her hand against the very slight curve of her tummy, there would be another child in the group. Boy or girl, she didn't mind. She was looking forward to telling Sergio her good news.

Lethally tall, dark and handsome in a dinner jacket, Sergio joined Kathy on the gallery at the top of the stairs. 'I love the dress. Gold is your colour. Is Ella asleep?'

'Yes, don't disturb her,' Kathy advised. 'She'll only start muttering about Elias again. They're a double act from hell. Ella's cheeky to him, he winds her up, she loses the plot and he laughs.'

Sergio tugged her into the shadows. 'Isn't that the way you are with me, *delizia mia*?'

Assailed by teasing dark golden eyes, Kathy laughed. 'Only when I first knew you. I've grown up quite a bit since then—'

'So you're not the woman who slammed down the phone on me last week when I couldn't get home in time for dinner?'

Kathy went pink with embarrassment and squirmed. 'Well, obviously that was an exception and I was in the wrong—'

'Oh, you can slam the phone down on me any time you like. I'm tough as granite,' Sergio husked, one hand splaying to her hip to curve her into connection with his long powerful thighs. 'And you said sorry very nicely in bed that night.'

Her guilty blush hit her hairline.

Sergio stared down at her with appreciative eyes. 'I love you, Kathy Torrente. You and Ella are the sunshine in my life—'

'And you're going to have to share that sunshine in the near future,' Kathy told him playfully, wanting to make her announcement before they joined their guests for the evening.

'You mean Horace, the most spoilt cat in Italy, is finally getting a mate?'

Kathy giggled like a drain. 'No, I'm pregnant!'

Warm satisfaction burnished his brilliant smile. 'You are an amazing woman.'

'I'm glad you think so.' Kathy locked her arms round his neck. Eventually they emerged from the shadows and she was lamenting that she would have to renew her lipstick. But she was laughing and he was watching her every lively change of expression with the intensity of a man very much in love. It was a while before they joined their guests…

Celebrate 100 years of pure reading pleasure with Mills & Boon®

To mark our centenary, each month we're publishing a special 100th Birthday Edition. These celebratory editions are packed with extra features and include a FREE bonus story.

Plus, starting in February you'll have the chance to enter a fabulous monthly prize draw. See 100th Birthday Edition books for details.

Now that's worth celebrating!

15th February 2008

Raintree: Inferno by Linda Howard
Includes FREE bonus story Loving Evangeline
A double dose of Linda Howard's heady mix of passion and adventure

4th April 2008

The Guardian's Forbidden Mistress by Miranda Lee
Includes FREE bonus story The Magnate's Mistress
Two glamorous and sensual reads from favourite author Miranda Lee!

2nd May 2008

The Last Rake in London by Nicola Cornick
Includes FREE bonus story The Notorious Lord
Lose yourself in two tales of high society and rakish seduction!

Look for Mills & Boon 100th Birthday Editions at your favourite bookseller or visit
www.millsandboon.co.uk

0108/CENTENARY_2-IN-1

4 FREE

BOOKS AND A SURPRISE GIFT!

We would like to take this opportunity to thank you for reading this Mills & Boon® book by offering you the chance to take FOUR more specially selected titles from the Modern™ series absolutely FREE! We're also making this offer to introduce you to the benefits of the Mills & Boon® Reader Service™—

- ★ **FREE home delivery**
- ★ **FREE gifts and competitions**
- ★ **FREE monthly Newsletter**
- ★ **Exclusive Reader Service offers**
- ★ **Books available before they're in the shops**

Accepting these FREE books and gift places you under no obligation to buy, you may cancel at any time, even after receiving your free shipment. Simply complete your details below and return the entire page to the address below. You don't even need a stamp!

YES! Please send me 4 free Modern books and a surprise gift. I understand that unless you hear from me, I will receive 6 superb new titles every month for just £2.99 each, postage and packing free. I am under no obligation to purchase any books and may cancel my subscription at any time. The free books and gift will be mine to keep in any case.

P8ZED

Ms/Mrs/Miss/Mr ....Initials ....

BLOCK CAPITALS PLEASE

Surname ....

Address ....

....

....Postcode..................

Send this whole page to:
UK: FREEPOST CN81, Croydon, CR9 3WZ